"Knight Errant Incorporated. Damsels in distress a speciality."

Oh, great. Not just a jack-the-lad who believed he was irresistible, but one who thought he was funny, too, Juliet thought as she opened the door to be confronted with six feet two inches of toned manhood wearing a worn leather bomber jacket and a pair of jeans that appeared to have been molded to his body.

His thick dark hair was too long, his grin too knowing, and his eyes a totally impossible shade of blue. The effect was aggressively male. Cocksure. Arrogant. And behind him, propped on a stand, was a motorbike to match.

Gregor McLeod, she realized, hadn't changed one bit. He was heavier, of course, but all of it was muscle, and there were lines carved into his cheeks, fanning out from his eyes, adding character to his youthful good looks. But he was still the same Gregor McLeod, and she had the weirdest feeling that as if by looking at her "wish-list" of goals and ambitions, she had conjured him up out of her past....

Liz Fielding started writing at the age of twelve, when she won a writing competition at school. After that early success there was quite a gap—during which she was busy working in Africa and the Middle East, getting married and having children—before her first book was published in 1992. Now readers worldwide fall in love with her irresistible heroes, and adore her independent-minded heroines. Visit Liz's Web site for news and extracts of upcoming books at www.lizfielding.com

Books by Liz Fielding

HARLEQUIN ROMANCE®
3798—A FAMILY OF HIS OWN
3817—THE BILLIONAIRE TAKES A BRIDE
3821—A SURPRISE CHRISTMAS PROPOSAL
3837—A WIFE ON PAPER

HER WISH-LIST BRIDEGROOM

Liz Fielding

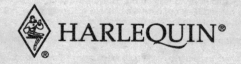

HARLEQUIN®

TORONTO • NEW YORK • LONDON
AMSTERDAM • PARIS • SYDNEY • HAMBURG
STOCKHOLM • ATHENS • TOKYO • MILAN • MADRID
PRAGUE • WARSAW • BUDAPEST • AUCKLAND

ISBN 0-373-03853-4

HER WISH-LIST BRIDEGROOM

First North American Publication 2005.

Copyright © 2004 by Liz Fielding.

PROLOGUE

'JULIET? Time to go.'

Glancing up from the figures she was checking, Juliet Howard smiled at the man framed in the doorway. Paul Graham was dressed in the standard executive uniform—dark suit, white shirt, discreetly striped tie—but on him they looked anything but standard. The man had the smouldering, chiselled good looks of a male model or an actor. Every office should have one, she thought as he closed the door and walked towards her.

Fortunately, this one was all hers—or at least he would be at the end of the month when his temporary secondment from the bank finished and her self-imposed rule of no relationships within the office would be over. Something that Paul had respected, with only the occasional—and flattering—display of impatience.

'I've told you not to do that in the office,' she chided as he leaned across her desk and kissed her, well aware that her attempt to appear stern was wasted on him.

He solemnly crossed his heart with his thumb. 'I swear I'll never do it again.'

That hadn't been quite the response she'd anticipated, but she waved him away with a, 'Make sure you don't.'

Instead of leaving, he reached out and wiped the edge of his thumb along her lip. 'I've smudged your lipstick. You'd better run along and fix it before you come to the boardroom. Our newly ennobled chairman wouldn't approve of messy lips.'

Their newly ennobled chairman made no secret of the fact that he believed women were useful only for breeding and the tedious work that men were too important to bother with. He did not like her and made no secret of the fact. Fortunately, she was too good at her job for him to find an excuse to be rid of her. She hoped he enjoyed his day, because once she'd delivered her plan for streamlining the transport arrangements of the company he was going to be seeing a lot more of her. 'Messy lipstick is going to be the least of his worries next week, but you're right, there's no point in aggravating the miserable old devil unnecessarily.' And she smiled.

She'd been smiling a lot lately. She'd arrived at Markham and Ridley, clutching her degree in business administration, seven years ago with one ambition. A seat on the board of one of the most old-fashioned and male dominated industries in the country. Stone, aggregates and all the products made from the hard stuff. The company had been coasting for years, relying on old licences to extract giving them a virtual monopoly in certain areas.

She'd done her research before joining them, had seen the possibilities and given herself ten years to achieve her goal.

Three months ago John Ridley had asked her to put together a paper, lay out her long-term plans for cutting costs, improving productivity. It was a recognised precursor to the offer of a directorship. On Monday she was going to deliver it.

She was within a whisker of having it all.

And not just the directorship—which proved she was

the equal of any man in the company. She had Paul, too—the most thoughtful, charming and attentive of men—proving that she was equal to any woman.

She had every right to smile. But this would not be a good day to be late. 'I'll just go and powder my nose. Grab a glass of champagne for me.'

'Yes, ma'am.'

She slipped a comb through her sleek, neat, conservative hairstyle—this was a very conservative company—and refreshed her lipstick. Tugged her jacket into place. Then the smile broke out again. It had been a tough journey, hard work, but it had paid off. She'd finally arrived.

The boardroom was already crowded when she opened the door and she couldn't immediately see Paul. She took a glass of champagne from the tray as she squeezed in, apparently the last to arrive, clearly having spent rather more time daydreaming about the success to come than she'd realised.

She had no time to think about it as the managing director tapped a glass for attention and raised a toast to their chairman. She took a sip and waited for the inevitable speech.

It was shorter than expected. But not nearly short enough.

'While I'm obviously delighted to have been honoured in this way, my greatest pleasure comes from an announcement I've been planning from the time I stood as his godfather thirty years ago.' He extended a hand and rested it on the shoulder of the man standing at his side. She craned around the person in front to see who it was.

Paul.

The expectant silence was only disturbed by a discreet rustle as two or three people glanced back to look at her.

Paul was Markham's godson? But why hadn't he told her?

'You all know Paul Graham,' he continued. 'He joined us a few months ago and has put that time to good use, studying how we do things. Now he's going to tell us how we can do it better. He'll be joining the board with immediate effect and will assume responsibility for implementing his plans to streamline the organisation and cut transport costs. A year from now Markham and Ridley will be fitter and leaner. A greyhound of a company that will leave the competition standing.'

The pause that followed this announcement went on just a little too long. And this time no one was looking at her. Not that she was noticing anything. She had eyes only for Paul.

His plan? Greyhound? That was a direct lift from her own paper...

What the devil was going on? What was Paul doing standing up there where she should be? Why wasn't he looking at her? This was a joke... It had to be a joke...

'Please raise your glasses and join me in a toast to Paul and to a bright future for all of us.'

No joke. Paul was Markham's godson. As he raised his glass, his lordship looked straight at her. He wasn't just smiling. He was positively smirking.

They both were, she realised.

As she stepped forward a path seemed to open in front of her and, for the first time in her life, Juliet Howard, the most careful girl in the world, the girl who'd planned her life down to the last comma and full stop, did something without thinking through the consequences.

There was no space in her mind to think. It was too busy fast-forwarding through every moment she'd spent in Paul's company. How he'd wooed her, how he'd made her feel safe and wanted without ever pressuring her. But had always been there from the first day she'd been asked to allow him to shadow her.

Right down to the Judas kiss he'd bestowed minutes earlier to delay her.

There was only one word to describe him and she used it, then flung the contents of her glass in his face.

CHAPTER ONE

'GET up, Jools.'

Juliet Howard heard her mother's voice but she didn't move. Packing her things—or rather watching her mother pack them—and the drive home to Melchester slumped in the passenger seat, had taken every scrap of energy she'd possessed. Getting out of bed was beyond her. It had been beyond her for weeks. Even the effort of opening her eyes was too much.

The sound of the curtains being drawn back heralded an implosion of light into the room. She turned away, burying her face in her pillow, trying to ignore the rattle of coat-hangers as her mother pulled out some clothes for her. Tossed them on the bed.

'I've written a shopping list. I didn't have time to shop this weekend so I've got nothing in. You might not care whether you eat or not, but I do. Put a move on and I'll drop you in town on my way to work. You can sign on at that job agency near the bus station after you've picked up my book from the Prior's Lane bookshop. Tell Maggie Crawford that I'll see her at bingo tonight.'

Her briskness was relentless.

Then, 'You should come, too.'

'To bingo?'

'Hallelujah! It speaks...'

Oh, right. She rolled over. Her mother wasn't serious about the bingo. She'd just thrown it in to get a response. 'Mum, you don't have to do this.'

'Convince me. Get up, take a shower, while I make some coffee.'

'You'll be late for work.'

'I will if you don't get a move on.'

'No...' But her mother, who had never been late for work in her entire life, didn't linger to argue. But then she never had. She'd never had the time for that. Had never allowed the fact that she was a single mother to give an employer the opportunity to say that she was unreliable. Had never once given in to self-pity, at least not when anyone was around to see. How many tears had she shed in the dark, lonely hours of the night?

Disgusted with herself, Juliet rolled over, allowing gravity to take her feet to the floor. The same technique that had got her out of bed on days when going to school had seemed like another day in purgatory.

The sun shining in at the window was an affront to her misery, the smell of coffee from the kitchen was making her feel sick, but her mother had surrendered her entire life, given all she knew and more to make sure her daughter had a chance of something better. Even now she was the one picking up the pieces. She had taken precious time off to go to London, had put her flat in the hands of a letting agent so that the mortgage would get paid, so that she'd have something to go back to. Had packed up and then brought her home and tucked her up in her childhood bed.

Even the teenager had been strong enough to get up, face the misery, counting each day she'd survived without attracting the attention of the school bullies a small bonus.

It wasn't strength now but guilt that propelled her into the shower, got her into the clothes laid out for her and, shivering, into the car. The sun was shining but it was still March and the wind was the lazy kind that didn't take the long way around but went right through you.

Her mother decanted her onto the pavement. 'Don't forget my book. And buy a bunch of daffodils from the market.'

She called at the job agency first, filled in the form they produced, sat while the woman behind the desk glanced over her qualifications, the steady advancement with her only employer since university.

'You haven't answered the question about why you left your last employer.'

'No.' Well, that was a tricky one. 'Sorry.' She took the form and wrote 'Bridget Jones Syndrome' and pushed it back across the desk.

'You shagged your boss?'

'No, I was the boss, but you know how it is with men. They always want to be on top.' It wasn't strictly true but it short-circuited the difficult questions. And she was sure that Paul would have made the sacrifice if she'd been less scrupulous, less careful of her career and reputation, less gullible…

'Oh, right.' She got a sympathetic look, but precious little else. 'You're a bit over-qualified for us, to be honest. The highest we go is junior execs. You really need a London agency.'

'I just want something temporary while I reassess my career options,' she said. Something the last specialist executive recruitment agency she'd contacted had suggested. They hadn't gone as far as asking her if it was true that she'd had a breakdown; they'd taken one look and drawn their own conclusions.

*   *   *

'What on earth persuaded you to buy this dump, Mac?'

Gregor McLeod looked around his latest acquisition with a certain amount of satisfaction. As a builder's yard it had had its day. Small places like this couldn't compete with the massive combined trade and DIY superstores that had sprung up on the business park at the edge of the city, but owning it had been high on his 'want' list for a long time.

'Just put it down to pure sentimentality, Neil. Once, in the dim and distant past, I worked here. Not for long, but I've never forgotten the experience.'

His deputy glanced around. 'I didn't know that.'

'Yes, well, you were away at university while I was sweating my guts out for Marty Duke, shifting loads that would have had Health and Safety screaming blue murder if they'd known.'

'Not exactly fond memories, then.'

'It wasn't all bad. There was a classy temp in the office. Long shiny hair, legs to the stratosphere and a voice as rich, smooth and expensive as Swiss chocolate. She had a smile that made coming to work a really worthwhile experience.'

Neil shook his head. 'What is it with you and posh birds, Mac? I'd have thought once bitten even you would have been twice shy.'

'Yes, well, in her case I wasn't on my own. She couldn't type in a straight line but Duke paid her well above the hourly rate because the builders used to line up to drool as she took their orders.'

'Why do I anticipate a sorry ending to this story?'

'Because you know me?' Greg shrugged. 'When I saw Duke with his hands where no employer should have them, I didn't bother to point out that sexual harassment in the workplace was inappropriate, I just decked him. He fired me while he was still lying flat on his back.'

'I hope the goddess with the expensive voice was suitably grateful.'

'Not noticeably, but then she was too busy playing Florence Nightingale to the boss. She must have made a really good job of it because he offered her a full-time position.'

'As his secretary?'

'No. His wife. I clearly misread the signals. She might have been up for a little hot necking in the stationery cupboard, but she had bigger ambitions than hooking up with a nineteen-year-old labourer with no prospects.'

Neil grinned as he looked around at the derelict yard. 'Her mistake.'

'You think so? I had nothing to offer her. She, on the other hand, did me a real favour. She taught me that when it comes to a choice between money and muscles women will choose money every time. And she showed me that I wasn't cut out to work for someone else.'

'So you bought a yard you don't need, saved Duke from going under, out of sheer gratitude to his wife? The woman to whom you owe your fortune?'

'I owe my fortune to hard work, a sharp eye for a good deal and a large measure of luck. I bought the yard for a number of reasons, the most pleasurable of which, I have to admit, was the fact that Duke had to look me in the eye and call me Mr McLeod.'

'What about his wife? Was she there?'

'She's still his secretary, would you believe?'

'I told you. It was a poor career move. What did she have to say?'

'Not much until she showed me to the door.' He pulled a face. 'Then she said, "Call me…"'

Juliet left the agency with the promise that 'if anything suitable came up' they'd call her. She'd done her best. Or the best that she was capable of right now. Tick one thing off the list, she thought, heading for the shops. The sooner she got the shopping done, the sooner she could go home.

She'd picked up her mother's basket without looking at the notebook lying in the bottom. Most women recycled old envelopes for shopping lists, but not her mother. She'd always used a notebook, not just for shopping lists, but for everything, maintaining that it freed the mind to think of more important things. And it made her feel good when she actually managed to tick an item off, especially the ones that began with the word 'pay…'

It was a habit she'd fostered in her daughter, encouraging her to write down not just the must-do everyday items such as prompts for handing in school projects, but developing one-year, five-year, ten-year plans.

And she'd told her she shouldn't just write down the big stuff because it got downright depressing when there were no new ticks. The thing was to write down absolutely everything because a person needed to see that she was achieving things, even if it was only remembering to buy a loaf of bread.

Picking up the ring-bound notebook, she realised it was an old one of hers. She'd had it in her stocking the Christmas she was twelve or thirteen. She remembered her pleasure in the glossy black cover with its bright red rings. Until then she'd had notebooks with

cute cats or hamsters or cartoon characters, but this one
seemed very grown up and so she'd carefully made a
label.

JULIET HOWARD
A MASTER PLAN FOR HER LIFE

The label was barely legible now and the gloss had
been rubbed off the cover from always being tucked
away at the bottom of her school bag safe from the
vicious prying of the school bullies.

She swallowed, aching for the lonely little girl she'd
been, and then, as someone pushed past her muttering
irritably about people with 'nothing better to do than
block the pavement,' she took refuge in a nearby café,
ordering coffee she didn't want in return for a quiet
space, somewhere to think.

What had that child yearned for?

She remembered the big plans, the ones that had
never altered. A place at a good university, a first class
honours degree, to one day be as successful as the
woman she'd seen opening a branch of her chain of
aromatherapy shops in the city.

Some things never changed.

Flipping through the pages as her coffee cooled, she
saw that she'd dutifully started her goals with getting
an A in maths, turning in her projects on time, keeping
her room tidy. But after that came the heartfelt goals—
the painful desire to have her hair cut really short so
that she could spike it up with gel like the 'cool' girls
at school. The yearning for impossibly expensive sports
shoes so that she would fit in. And then there was the

holiday at Disneyworld in Paris. Had she really wanted to go, or was it on the list because it had seemed as if it was something everyone else in her year had done? Even the ones from single parent homes, like her. Because not going marked her out as a 'loser' in the eyes of the other girls.

Whatever, like so many of the dreams, it had never been ticked.

There was nothing to stop her packing her bags and going right now, of course. But really, it was too pathetic to go to Disneyworld without children of her own with whom to share the magic.

She saw she'd planned on four of her own—a reflection of her 'only child' desire for brothers and sisters, no doubt. She hadn't specified who would be their father at the time.

That was the last item on the list. Just before the book had been abandoned. That was the problem with having a master plan. It was an upwards progression. Life, on the other hand, was a game of Snakes and Ladders.

She turned the page. The shopping list had not been written in the notebook, but was on a yellow peel-off note. Clearly the notebook had been her mother's not entirely subtle way of reminding her that her life hadn't come to an end simply because the goal she'd set herself had shifted from the 'achievable' to the 'downright impossible' level.

You just had to start a fresh list. Write a new five-year plan. As for those impossible dreams…

'One step at a time, Mother,' she muttered to herself, dropping the book back into the basket.

There was nothing too taxing on the shopping list. Nothing that she couldn't have got from the eight-till-late on the corner. Except the book—which could easily have waited until another day. And the daffodils—specified, no doubt, because of their hideously cheerful yellowness.

She compromised by buying some paper-white narcissi from a stallholder in the little market at the bottom of Prior's Lane and then headed in the direction of the bookshop.

The sooner she got everything the sooner she could go home.

And then what? Stare at four walls and feel sorry for herself? Had her mother ever behaved so pitifully? Why on earth was she being so kind? Why wasn't she telling her to pull herself together and get over it?

She glanced at the notebook lying in the bottom of the basket. Okay. Her mother was. Or at least suggesting that it was time she wrote herself a new list. Item one would be easy enough. Stop feeling sorry for herself.

Except that wasn't how it worked. They had to be real things that you could tick off. Okay. Item one. Find a job.

Then she'd be too busy to feel sorry for herself.

Unfortunately no one in their right mind was going to employ a senior manager who'd ruined the chairman's big day by drowning him and his protégé in champagne.

Stress! That wasn't stress. It was a lot simpler than that…

After that it got a bit silly. While mentally compiling a list of all the terrible things she wanted to do to Lord Markham and his wretched godson had a certain cathartic effect, they were downright impossible. The whole point was to be able to cross things off so that you felt as if you'd achieved something. Felt better.

Which put a stop to her list making. Feeling better was not going to happen anytime soon.

She stopped, looked around to check where she was. Prior's Lane curved up the hill from the river to the cathedral. It wasn't just one street but a network of narrow lanes and alleys that had once been the medieval heart of the city, a world away from the sterile, traffic-free shopping area in the city centre where look-alike chain stores meant you could be in any town, anywhere.

It had once provided shopping on a human scale with exciting little shops and smart boutiques and the air had been redolent with the scent of freshly roasted coffee. Now the predominance of charity shops was a sure indication of an area past its use-by date. Even the shops that were clinging on were in dire need of a coat of paint.

She felt a jag of irritation at such a waste of a resource. What was the City Council thinking of? She'd been to other cities where places like this were thriving tourist haunts making a valuable contribution to the style and financial well-being of the area.

It wasn't all bad news. Maybe it was the unaccustomed exercise, the surge of healthy anger, but the scent of freshly baked bread sparked a sudden hunger and once she'd bought a crusty French loaf, still warm from the oven, it seemed perfectly natural to add a small piece of Dolcelatte and some fat olives—her mother loved them and she deserved a treat—from an old-fashioned Italian mama-and-papa grocer's.

In the part of London where she'd lived—until she'd tossed away her career along with the contents of her champagne glass—shops like these would have been packed out with foodie fanatics fighting over the freshly made pasta and virgin olive oil. Here everyone seemed to be hanging on by the skin of their teeth.

A bell jangled as she opened the bookshop door. It was exactly as she remembered it. No concessions to the new age of book selling. No coffee, no snacks, no armchairs, no incentive to linger.

She did, however, find the Cornwell her mother had put on the list and a Paretsky that she hadn't—her mother preferred crime novels with strong female heroines—and she picked that up too. Then, since no one had appeared to take her money, she called out. 'Hello?'

There was no answer so she made her way around some shelves dividing the front from the back of the shop and blinked at the array of sofas and armchairs, the fact that back here the shelves were stacked with used books.

Then, approaching the small office at the rear, 'Hello? Mrs Crawford? Is there anyone...'

And that was when she saw Maggie Crawford stretched out on the floor, an overturned chair lying nearby telling its own story.

She was so pale that for one terrible moment Juliet thought she was dead and her first reaction was fear. Panic. The shaming impulse to bolt and leave someone else to find her, deal with it.

An overwhelming 'I can't' and 'Why me?' response.

Then, dropping everything, she ran to help. 'Mrs Crawford? Can you hear me?'

She opened her eyes, looking vaguely surprised and said, 'Oh, hello, dear. It's Juliet, isn't it? Your mother said you might drop in...' Her voice was weak, but at least she was making sense. Then she said, 'What on earth am I doing down here?'

'No!' Juliet put her hand on the woman's shoulder as she moved to sit up. 'No, you just stay there. You've had a fall.' And she dug her phone out of her pocket and dialled the emergency services, unfastening her coat, switching hands so that she could slip her arms through the sleeves and lay it over the woman to keep her warm, as she explained what had happened to the dispatcher.

'It's Mrs Crawford. Mrs Margaret Crawford. The bookshop, Prior's Lane…'

'Oh, dear. What a nuisance I'm being.'

'Nonsense, Maggie.' She replaced the receiver and knelt at her side, taking her hands, chafing them between her own. 'Just hold on, help is on its way. How long have you been lying here?'

'I don't know, dear. I just wanted to fix a piece of card in the window,' she said. 'To block the draught. I was reaching up and then I felt dizzy and the next thing—'

'Shh—'

'No. You don't understand. I can't leave it like that…'

She was beginning to get fractious and Juliet, looking up, saw that one of the panes was broken near the catch. It had all the hallmarks of an attempted burglary. At least she assumed it was just an attempted burglary. The office didn't look as if it had been ransacked.

She saw a small electric fire and turned it on to counteract the cold air coming through the window, then, in an effort to reassure her, keep her still, said, 'Don't worry. I'll sort something out, get it fixed, just as soon as—' She heard the shop door open.

'Hello? Did someone call for help?'

'Through here.' It was with considerable relief that she handed responsibility for the patient over to the paramedics. First aid had never been one of her strong points.

The window, on the other hand, was something she could fix. Or at least she could find someone who could do the job for her. There was a hardware shop across the way. The sign outside boasted that it was an 'old-fashioned store with old-fashioned service' and in truth it looked like something out of a working museum. It seemed like a good moment to put that 'old-fashioned service' ethic to the test. 'It'll be a few minutes before you can move her, won't it?' she asked the paramedic. 'I want to organise someone to fix the window. She's fretting—'

'Maybe you could do it after we've gone, Miss. We need a few details, if you don't mind.'

'But...' No. Obviously someone had to stay until the window was fixed, and there wasn't a queue forming. Just her. 'Of course.' She gave them her name, answered what questions she could, while one of them made Maggie more comfortable.

The shop doorbell jingled again. When she didn't move, the one asking the questions smiled and said, 'Okay, I think that's all we need from you, Miss. You can see to your customer if you like.'

About to say, *No...* I'm *the customer,* she let it go. Someone had to go and explain that the shop was temporarily shut, put up the Closed sign.

'I'm sorry,' she began as she approached the woman who was standing by the cash desk and searching through her bag for something. 'I'm afraid there's no one here to serve you just at the moment—'

'I don't need serving. I've just come to pick up a book I ordered. It's paid for,' she said, handing over a receipt as proof. Then, when she was clearly at a loss, 'Maggie usually keeps special orders under the desk.'

'Does she? Oh, right. Is this it?' She held up a thick paperback, a historical romance. There were several more copies obviously waiting to be picked up. 'It seems to be a popular book.'

'It's the romance reading group choice for next month. Maggie always orders them in for us.'

'Oh, I see.' She placed it in a carrier bag and handed it to her, making a note of what she'd done on the notepad beside the phone.

'Been taken poorly, has she?' the woman asked, in no great hurry to leave. 'Maggie?'

Pointless to deny it with the ambulance blocking the lane in front of the shop. 'She's had a fall.'

'Nasty.' She shook her head. 'She's not a young woman and it shakes you up, something like that. You lose your confidence. If she's broken something I imagine it'll be the end of another Prior's Lane shop.'

'Surely not?'

'Who's going to take it on? These little shops can't compete, can they? It's cheaper to buy the bestsellers in the supermarket, which is okay if all you want to read is bestsellers.' She patted the carrier with the paperback in it. 'You won't find anything like this on their shelves at three for the price of two.'

'No, I suppose not.'

She could probably have bought the Cornwell at the supermarket but it was unlikely they'd stock the Paretsky...

'Okay, Miss Howard, we're bringing her through. If

you ring Melchester General in a couple of hours there should be some news for you.'

'Oh, but—' She let it go. Her own concerns were unimportant. 'Maggie, is there someone you'd like me to contact for you?'

'You will take care of the window?' she asked, her mind apparently fixed on that. 'They will keep breaking them…' It was clearly an effort for her to speak and Juliet didn't press it. It wouldn't be any trouble to get the window fixed and she'd probably be able to find a contact number for someone in the office.

'I'll see to it, then I'll lock up and come in to see you later.'

'Poor dear,' her customer said, as she was loaded into the ambulance. 'She's only got her son and he's working out in the Middle East somewhere.' *Oh, great!* And having dropped that little bombshell, 'Well, I must get on. Good luck.'

'But—'

It occurred to her that she'd said 'but' more times in the last half an hour than she had in the last seven years. Her usual response to a problem was to say, *No problem.*

Angry with herself for being so pathetic, she turned the sign on the door to Closed and slipped the catch. There was 'no problem.' All she had to do was find a glazier for the window, find someone who could take responsibility for the shop and then go to the hospital to reassure Maggie that everything was taken care of.

That was all. A piece of cake for someone with her experience and ability. She sank down on to a stool behind the counter. Window… Glazier…

She pulled herself together. The hardware shop.

First she had to find the shop keys. She could hardly

walk out and leave it unlocked and, if she locked the door behind her, she wouldn't be able to let the glazier in to do the work.

She finally found the shop keys in the desk drawer at the back of the shop but, halfway to the door, she changed her mind and decided to phone them in case whoever had tried to break in had simply been disturbed and, having seen Maggie carried out, was hanging around, waiting for another chance at the till.

Pulling the telephone directory towards her, she realised that she'd have to do something about the till, too. Secure the money. She reached for a pen and, with a certain sense of irony, she fished her notebook out of the basket and began to make a list.

'So what *are* you going to do with the yard?'

Greg looked out of the filthy office windows at the deserted builder's yard, wondering what had happened to the men who'd worked there. 'It's not just this dump. The deal included the freehold on some retail property in the old part of the city.'

'Oh, great. Low rents, high maintenance.' The phone began to ring and as he reached for it Neil said, 'Leave it. Duke's Yard is no longer trading—'

'Duke's Yard,' Greg answered.

'And besides,' Neil continued, but with the resignation of a man who knew he was talking to himself, 'it's lunchtime.'

'Oh, thank goodness. I got your number from the hardware shop in Prior's Lane, but they weren't sure you were still…'

Greg, his attention suddenly wholly engaged on the voice in his ear, ignored Neil, instead propping himself on the edge of the desk. Some days weren't just good—

'Still what?' he prompted.

'In business.' When he didn't confirm or deny it she said, 'Obviously he was mistaken.' Greg said nothing. 'Fortunately.' Then, 'Look, this is an emergency. Can you help?'

'Try me,' he offered.

There was the slightest pause before she said, 'Right, well, I have a small window-pane that needs replacing as a matter of urgency. Is there any chance of you sending 'round someone to do it today?'

—some days were perfect, he decided.

'What time today?'

'The sooner the better. I'm in Prior's Lane. The bookshop?'

'I know it. And your name?'

'Howard.'

'Really? You don't sound like a Howard. You sound more like an Emma or a Sophie or—'

'Juliet Howard.'

'Or a Juliet.' There was the slightest sound that might just have been a choked off suggestion of disbelief. 'I'm sorry, did you say something?'

'No. Look, can you do it because if you can't—'

She sounded as if she was at, or at least very near, the end of her tether. 'And your telephone number, Juliet?'

'Why do you need my telephone number?'

'Because, oddly enough, some people think it's amusing to call out workmen on completely phoney jobs. I make a point of calling back to double check.'

She obviously decided that she had no choice because, after a momentary hesitation, she gave him the number.

He made a note of it and said, 'I'll be with you in ten minutes.'

'Really?' She sounded as if she was torn between incredulity and relief, with incredulity winning by a nose.

Neil frantically shook his head, pointing at his watch as he mouthed the word, 'Lunch.'

Greg grinned and mouthed back, 'Swiss chocolate.' Then, into the phone, 'Is that a problem?' he asked.

'No, I'll be here,' she replied, but he got the distinct impression that she wouldn't be holding her breath.

'So,' Neil grumbled as he replaced the receiver, 'she's got a voice like expensive chocolate. She's probably got a blue rinse, twin set and pearls to go with it.'

Greg shrugged. 'If you're right I'll have done my good deed for the day. If you're wrong…'

'If I'm wrong?'

There had been a crisp edge to her voice, exactly like the snap of the finest chocolate, along with a just a touch of melting vulnerability as she'd uttered that disbelieving, 'Really?'

Irresistible.

'You know me, Neil. I believe in playing my luck while it's running with me.'

'Luck! First you land us with an expensive waste of space and then you decide to abandon a working lunch on the off chance that this bird's face fits her voice.'

'Faint heart…' he replied. 'And it's my expensive waste of space, not yours.'

Neil's response was short and scatological.

'Okay, make that my expensive space that's going to be included in the new development zone.'

'You—' Then, 'Duke didn't know about that, did he?'

'I certainly didn't tell him.' Then, 'Since you won't be having a long lunch at my expense you can use the time to find out what happened to his workforce. If any of them are out of work, see what we can do for them.'

'Oh, for heaven's sake!' Juliet flipped her mobile shut and tossed it on the desk. *Try me*… Not in this lifetime. The very last thing she needed was some jack-the-lad who thought he was the answer to every woman's prayer.

Not that she could afford to be fussy.

Duke's Yard had been the last number on her list and 'jack' was the only one who could do it this week, let alone today. She wouldn't tick it off her list just yet though. Despite his promise, he hadn't called back.

And, even if he did turn up, she was firmly crossing her fingers that his availability meant he had a brief window in his busy schedule, not that he was so useless no one would employ him. Fortunately it wasn't anything cerebrally demanding, such as electrical wiring or plumbing, that needed doing. How difficult could it be to replace a small pane of glass in a window? She could probably do it herself if she knew where to go for the glass, had the tools, the putty…

She realised that her hands were shaking. There was a tiny kitchenette next to the office and she found the kettle, filled it at the sink and switched it on before looking around for a jar of coffee.

She was spooning some into a mug when there was another in a long series of knocks and rattles as, ignoring the Closed sign, hopeful customers still tried the front door. The shop might not be warm and well-lit with the inviting scent of coffee, but it didn't seem to be short of people trying to get in.

Whether they were actually desperate to purchase a book or just curious about why the ambulance had been there she didn't know and didn't have much trouble resisting the temptation to find out.

Then, as she poured the boiling water on to the coffee, it occurred to her that it might—however unlikely it might seem—possibly be 'jack' coming to fix the window. A whole minute early. How likely was that?

She went to check anyway.

By the time she'd walked through to the front of the shop whoever it was had given up. On the point of unlocking the door to check outside, she heard another knock, this time at the back door. Unlike the shop door it was made of solid wood rather than glass and before she opened up caution prompted her to call out, 'Who's there?'

'Knight Errant Incorporated. Damsels in distress a speciality.'

Oh, great. Not just a jack-the-lad who believed he was irresistible but one who thought he was funny, too. She supposed she should be thankful that he'd resisted the more obvious 'Romeo' she decided as she opened the door to be confronted with six feet two inches of toned manhood wearing a worn leather bomber jacket and a pair of jeans that appeared to have been moulded to his body.

His thick, dark hair was too long, his grin too knowing and his eyes a totally impossible shade of blue. The effect was aggressively male. Cocksure. Arrogant. And behind him, propped on a stand, was a motorbike to match.

Gregor McLeod, she realised, hadn't changed one bit.

CHAPTER TWO

JULIET'S mouth dried and for a moment she couldn't think of a thing to say. All she could think, hope, pray, was that he wouldn't remember her.

'I am in the right place?' he prompted finally, breaking the long silence. How could she not have recognised his voice? Soft, gravelly and far too sexy for common decency... 'The bookshop? You did call Duke's Yard about a broken window?' And he glanced up at the window as if to say, *Well, one of us knows what they're talking about.*

So that was all right.

There wasn't the slightest sign of recognition.

As far as she knew he'd never known her name; he'd always called her 'princess,' for which she'd been teased mercilessly, although never in his hearing.

And back then she'd been a skinny thirteen-year-old in charity shop clothes, metal-framed glasses—years before Harry Potter made them fashionable—and with her long hair in a childish plait, quietly shadowing her hero around the school.

Except, of course, he hadn't been a hero.

A hero wouldn't have just disappeared from her life without a word.

'Yes.' She pulled herself together, ignoring the little tug of disappointment that while he'd made such a major impact on her, she hadn't even dented his memory. Refusing to regret that she hadn't made more effort with her appearance. Put on a little make-up. Done more than twist her hair up and impale it with a few pins. 'Yes, this is the bookshop. But I don't need a knight errant,' she said, at last finding her tongue and having no difficulty in resisting the 'irresistible rogue' look now she was old enough to recognise it for what it was. 'I need a glazier, or at least someone who can replace the glass in that.' She stepped out into the access lane that ran along the back of the shops to indicate the broken pane, bending down to pick up a piece of jagged glass, rather than continue staring at him.

She'd already seen enough.

'Leave that.' He bent beside her, taking the glass from her fingers.

Startled, she looked up.

'You'll cut yourself.'

'Oh, right. Thank you.' No. He hadn't changed at all. He was heavier, of course, but all of it was muscle and there were lines carved into his cheeks, fanning out from his eyes, adding character to his youthful good looks. But he was still the same Gregor McLeod and she had the weirdest feeling that, by looking at her list of goals, ambitions, she had conjured him up out of her past.

'I'd like it done today,' she said, standing up and brushing the dust of the lane from her fingers.

'If you're hinting that I didn't get here in the ten minutes I promised,' he replied, ignoring her snippy tone, 'then blame yourself. If you'd bothered to open the shop door when I knocked I'd have been a full thirty seconds early.'

'Oh, was that you?' She hadn't asked him in, hadn't actually been aware of standing back to let him past, but he was, nevertheless, inside the office and making it feel uncomfortably small. His closeness raising the hair on the nape of her neck, goosing her skin... 'I assumed—'

'You assumed that when I said "ten minutes" I was being over-optimistic?'

'Well, yes.' Then, realising that might not have been the wisest thing to have said, 'No! You were very prompt. I meant that I assumed you were a customer.'

'So you ignored it? I don't want to tell you how to run your business, Juliet, but you won't sell many books that way.'

'You're absolutely right,' she replied, straining for politeness. 'But then I don't sell books.'

'Well, there you are. Point made,' he said, the grin deepening as he made himself at home, propping his perfectly formed backside on the corner of the desk.

Oh, puh-lease...

Some men couldn't help it. They looked at a woman and whether they fancied her or not—and she was quite sure that she was no more his 'type' than he was hers now she knew better—they just had to flex their 'pulling' muscles.

Well, he was wasting his time on her.

Working her way to the top in a man's world, she'd quickly learned that the only way to deal with his kind was to remain calm and businesslike. Never to show by even the smallest twitch that she was aware of any sexual overture.

You might get the reputation for being a frigid cow, but there were worse things.

Stupidity, for instance.

Gullibility...

Mercifully his kind had a very short attention span; they knew that if one woman didn't respond to the muscle-flexing and chest-beating there'd be another one along in a minute.

It was the quiet men, the ones with brains, that you had to watch.

'I was waiting for you to call and check back that I wasn't some teenager playing a stupid prank,' she said.

'No teenager ever sounded like you, princess.'

She swallowed. Clamped down hard on her jaw to cut off the ridiculous stinging at the back of her eyes. Clearly he called every woman he met 'princess.' So much easier than all that bother of having to remember their names.

'Can you handle the job?' she demanded. Then, realising that probably sounded sharper than was entirely prudent, 'I mean can you handle it today?'

'That's what I'm here for.'

'Right,' she said. 'Good.' Then, 'How long will it take?'

'Well, let's see. I'll measure the window, go and get a piece of glass cut and then, while I clean this out and fit it, you can make me a cup of tea—top of the milk, two sugars—and tell me the story of your life.'

'How long?' she repeated, in the same even tone.

He seemed to find that amusing. At least she assumed that was why he was grinning.

'An hour should do it. Depending on how interesting your life has been until now.'

Oh, joy. A whole hour of flirtatious backchat. 'And how much will an hour of your time cost?'

'Why don't you just buy me lunch and we'll call it quits?'

And he had the nerve to criticise her lack of business sense?

'I'll fetch you a steak from the butcher on the corner, shall I? I imagine you do eat it raw?'

He took a steel tape from his pocket and reached up to measure the window—and he didn't need to stand on a chair. 'You know,' he said, his back to her, 'I had a date this lunchtime. I was just on my way out when you rang. I could have told you I was busy.'

'Why didn't you?' she asked. 'Everyone else did.'

'You sounded as if you needed help.'

She refused to be seduced by his apparent empathy. 'I did. I do. But I need a glazier not a chat-up line so why don't you save time by leaving out the tea and the life story? Call your date.' She refused to succumb to the flutter of jealousy, the 'Who?' and 'Where?' that flashed through her brain. 'I'm sure she'd wait for half an hour.'

'Would you?' he asked, glancing back over his shoulder. 'Wait?'

Ignoring the disconcerting way her pulse kicked into overdrive, she said, 'I wouldn't have agreed to have lunch with you in the first place so the occasion would never arise.'

'Consider the question hypothetically.'

This was her fault. She'd broken the cardinal rule— never get involved with someone in the office. Six months ago, three months even, and she could have handled this kind of conversation without losing her cool. Even with Gregor McLeod.

But her cool had been permanently blown by Paul's callous pretence and no matter how much she tried to keep it pinned down, anger would keep breaking through the miasma of misery like little puffs of sulphurous smoke warning that a volcano is about to blow.

'Hypothetically?' she repeated.

Ice cool. Mill pond calm. Duchess polite—no, *princess* polite. She could do it if she tried.

'That's what I said.'

'Then, hypothetically,' she replied, 'I'd say that if I had agreed to have lunch with you and you called to explain that you'd be late because you were helping a damsel in distress...' She stopped, seeing the trap a fraction of a second too late.

'Go on,' he said, but not making much of an effort to hide his amusement.

'I'm sure you'll think of something.'

'You wouldn't be suggesting that I've had a lot of practice in making excuses, would you?'

'You can't help it,' she said, deciding that since cool, calm and polite weren't doing the trick, she might as well go for natural. Whatever that was these days. 'You're a man. The excuse mechanism comes ready packaged with the chromosomes.' She listened to the words coming out of her mouth with a certain amount of horrified fascination. For a woman who, until a few months ago, hadn't taken a single risk in her life, had kept her emotions locked up for so long that she'd forgotten where she'd put the key, she seemed to have suddenly lost the plot.

Fortunately her knight errant was fully occupied writing down the window measurements in the notebook he'd taken from the buttoned down pocket of his cream wool shirt. It looked just like her notebook. The shiny black cover worn dull with use. It would be warm from his body, she thought. Full of his thoughts...

'Please accept that I'm deeply appreciative of your sacrifice,' she went on quickly in an effort to distract herself.

That did provoke a reaction. Nothing excessive. Just some slight movement of an eyebrow suggesting he wasn't totally impressed by her declaration of appreciation, no matter how deep.

'I would, however, be grateful if you'd get on with the job so that we can both get on with our lives,' she concluded, primly. 'I assume you do have one.'

'Do you?'

He looked up, regarded her thoughtfully, and it occurred to her that it would be a lot wiser to stick to the job. Personal remarks simply gave him an open invitation to develop his chat-up technique.

When she didn't answer, he said, 'The thing is, I like to show an interest in my customers. Get to know them. Build up a rapport.'

'Very commendable.' That was better. Suitably distant. 'I promise that if I should ever need someone to fix a pane of glass in the future, Duke's Yard is the first name that will come into my head.'

'Sarcasm is not attractive in a woman, Juliet.'

Sarcasm? That wasn't sarcasm. 'Well, thank you—'

She pulled herself up short. He was using her name in an attempt to get her to ask his. The truth was that she'd just come very close to using it without thinking. If she did that he'd want to know how she knew it and, while it probably wouldn't embarrass him one bit that he didn't remember her—and why should it?—she'd be embarrassed beyond bearing if he discovered that she'd never forgotten him. Because he wouldn't need the reason spelled out in words of one syllable. He'd know why.

'I'll be sure and make a note of that useful advice,' she continued, 'and stick it up somewhere I'll see it every day.'

Now *that* was sarcasm, she congratulated herself. Then, in the moment of silence that followed this pronouncement, when her words seemed to echo around the room, she realised that he was right.

It was not attractive.

Not that it deterred him.

'So, what happened to Maggie Crawford?' he asked. 'Have you taken over the shop?'

'No.'

'You're working for her?'

'Not even that.'

'Pity. This place could do with something to brighten it up.'

On that she agreed with him, but she wasn't about to admit it. As for her brightening anything...

'Maggie fell off a chair this morning. She was trying to stuff a piece of cardboard into the window to keep out the draught. She's been taken to the hospital.'

'I'm sorry to hear that.' He was deeply convincing. She almost believed him. 'So, what's your connection?'

He just wouldn't quit. 'Don't you have to go and fetch some glass?' she enquired.

'You know, I'm feeling distinctly peckish. Maybe you're right. I could still catch...'

'No!'

'No?'

'Look, I'm sorry, but it's been a trying morning. I just came in here to pick up a book for my mother. I found Maggie lying on the floor.'

'And you stayed to sort out the window?' he asked, looking around and catching her watching him. 'For someone you don't know?' And without warning the blue eyes looked dangerous rather than laddish.

'She was concerned. Agitated. And I do know her. At least, my mother does. I used to come in here when I was at school. She used to let me sit quietly out the back and read the books I couldn't afford to buy.'

'I see. I'm sorry. It's just occurred to me that you probably need to get back to work.'

'No, you're all right. I'm between jobs.'

'There's going to be a vacancy here, by the look of things. A temporary one, anyway.'

'Yes, well, I'll ask Mrs Crawford what she wants me to do about that when she's fit enough to talk about it. In the meantime I could hardly leave the shop open to the elements. Or any passing felon hoping to find a rare first edition of that popular classic, *The Beginners Guide to Successful Breaking and Entering*,' she added.

He was *supposed* to grin at that. Laddish she could deal with. Instead he looked thoughtful, glancing back up at the window.

'I doubt this was done by someone hoping to brush up on his lock-picking skills. More likely it was someone attempting to break in to the pharmacy next door.'

'An out-of-his-mind junkie looking for a fix?' Maggie had said it kept happening... 'Oh, great. That makes me feel so much easier in my mind.'

'You could stick a notice on the window,' he offered. 'Something along the lines of "This is a bookshop. Please break in next door..."'

'I'm sure the pharmacist would really appreciate that.'

'He'll have much better security,' he said, heading for the door. 'I'll go and fetch the glass. Why don't you see if you can round up a couple of chocolate Hobnobs to go with the tea since lunch has been cancelled? It's been a long time since breakfast.'

'This is a bookshop not a grocery store...' But once he'd decided to go he hadn't hung around and she was talking to herself, with nothing but the pheromone-laden atmosphere and the throaty roar of a motorbike to account for her raised pulse rate.

Gregor McLeod was a throw-back to the Dark Ages, she decided. Positively Neanderthal. How she could ever have thought he was... Well, it didn't matter what she'd thought. He did at least appear to know what he was doing. And he had come when he'd said he would. Maybe she shouldn't have been quite so hard on him.

On the other hand, he clearly didn't need any encouragement and, making sure the door was not just shut but locked, she settled at the desk with her luke-warm coffee and flicked through Maggie's Rolodex looking, without success, for her son's address.

She went through the desk diary, too, but that didn't prove any more illuminating and there was no sign of Maggie's handbag. It would have to wait until she went up to the hospital. She must have a neighbour or friend who could take in some personal things.

Someone who could take responsibility for the bookshop.

Then, when her stomach reminded her that it had indeed been a long time since breakfast—not that she'd actually eaten any breakfast—she looked at her watch and realised just how much time had passed since her knight errant had departed. Terrific. He'd probably had a better offer. Or he'd decided to put his lunch date before her cry for help. She could hardly blame him when she'd been so...sarcastic.

She sighed. She really shouldn't have let him get to her. He wasn't responsible for her childish hero-worship of him. Well, he was, but all he'd done was pick her up when she'd been pushed over. Had set her on her feet. Picked up her things, and by that one act of kindness, kept the bullies at bay for months. They'd only returned to bait her when he'd disappeared…

She glanced at the window. If he didn't return soon she'd be the one climbing on that decidedly wobbly chair and trying to jam a piece of cardboard into the gap.

What joy…

She left it while she rang the hospital, pretending to be a relative of Maggie's. There was no news beyond the fact that Mrs Crawford had been admitted and was 'comfortable.'

Her coffee had gone cold so she made another cup. Then, realising that she was hungrier than she'd been in weeks, she tore a lump off the end of the French bread, found a knife in the minuscule kitchen and slathered it with the creamy Dolcelatte.

She'd just bitten into it when there was a sharp rap on the back door. Bearing in mind the fact that there might still be a junkie in pain out there she didn't leap to open it but, mouth full of bread and cheese, managed a fairly fierce, 'Whooth at…?'

'Juliet?'

She opened the door. 'Thorry,' she said, gesturing with the bread she was still holding. 'Unch.'

'Thanks,' he said, taking it from her as if she'd offered it to him. 'I'm starving. You know, for a minute there I thought your burglar had returned and gagged you to blunt your sharp tongue.'

'My thung isn'th tharp…' she declared in an outraged shower of crumbs.

His response was to bite into the bread and cheese. Oh, terrific…

She stopped, chewed, swallowed. 'What took you so long?' she demanded when she could speak properly.

He'd used the time to finish her lunch and, after sucking some cheese from his thumb, said, 'Since that window is so easily accessible I had a look around the yard for something a bit more substantial than a pane of glass as a deterrent. Hold the door will you, while I bring the stuff in?'

Stuff?

'What stuff?'

He didn't answer, just opened the rear doors of a small scruffy van with Duke's Yard painted on the side and handed her a box that according to the label contained a burglar alarm kit.

'No. Wait...' He glanced at her. 'I can't...'

'Can't what?'

What on earth was the matter with her? She was dithering like a girl on her first day at work. Not that she'd dithered even then. She'd known exactly what she wanted—it was all on the list—and had been determined to get there.

No, she was dithering like a girl who'd been set on her feet by the sexiest boy in school. The boy every girl wanted to be noticed by. Even skinny girls with glasses...

'Look, I'm sorry Mr... Knight.' Oh, that felt so *good*. 'Mr...Errant. Or are you Mr Duke?' she enquired innocently.

'Now you're just being insulting,' he said. 'My name—since you're asking—is McLeod. Gregor McLeod,' he elaborated when she took rather longer than usual to respond.

'Really?' she said, snapping back to the present. 'I must have misheard you before.' Then, 'I'm sorry, Mr

McLeod, but I'm not in a position to sanction that amount of expense on Mrs Crawford's behalf.'

'Greg or Mac,' he said. 'Only people I don't like are required to call me Mister. And who said anything about expense? Buy me dinner and we'll call it even.'

Well, he had his priorities sorted. One pane of glass equalled lunch. A burglar alarm was worth dinner. She didn't want to know what she'd be expected to barter for the metal window grille he was lifting out of the van.

'On the other hand, I'm sure it would make her mind easier if she knew her premises were safely secured,' she said.

'Dinner would be cheaper,' he said, following her inside.

Not in her experience.

'I'm really not interested, Mr McLeod.'

'Women usually call me Greg,' he said, elaborating on the name thing. 'Or Gregor.'

'I only call people I like by their first name,' she replied, 'but I'm happy to drop the Mister if it offends you.' And, just to show him that it wasn't anything personal, she smiled and said, 'I'll make you that cup of tea now, McLeod.'

'You're all heart,' he said, reaching into his jacket, 'but I have the feeling I was well advised to bring my own chocolate biscuits.'

He handed her the packet, warm from his body.

'Lovely,' she said, holding the packet unenthusiastically at arm's length, as if it might bite. She just knew the chocolate was going to stick to her fingers when she opened it and that she wouldn't be able to resist licking them. Once she'd done that...

No. She'd done the night of shame with chocolate

and she dropped the packet on the desk out of harm's way. If he wanted them, he'd have to open it himself.

'I'm a really cheap date,' he assured her.

'I'll bear that in mind.' Realising that he was looking at her expectantly, that her heart lifted in response to his steady flax-blue gaze in just the same way as it had done all those years ago, she added cruelly, 'If I should ever need a cheap date.'

She left him to it and went into the little kitchenette to fill the kettle at the sink indicating that as far as she was concerned the exchange was at an end and she'd appreciate him getting on with the job.

Not that she expected him to be put off that easily. Surprised—and if she was honest just the tiniest bit disappointed—when he didn't come back with some outrageous comment, she glanced back over her shoulder.

He'd taken off his jacket and, as she looked, he peeled off his shirt to reveal a T-shirt that clung like a second skin. Only a man who wanted to display his Tarzan credentials would wear such a garment, even to work, she thought. Or a man who didn't understand the temperature control on his washing machine. Pathetic on both counts. But his lack of repartee was explained by the fact that he was concentrating on removing the broken pieces of glass from the window.

As he reached up the muscles on his shoulders bunched and rippled and the T-shirt rode up, threatening to expose an inch or two of flesh at his waist.

Realising that she was holding her breath in anticipation—she might be off the entire male half of the population but she wasn't dead—she quickly turned away and switched on the kettle before going through to the shop where she made herself useful tidying the

books on the 'new titles' table. Flipping through the
unopened post to see if there was anything that looked
urgent and giving herself a moment to recover from the
unexpected rush of mindless lust that had caught her
by surprise.

She didn't do mindless anything, but even she had
to admit that the sheer physicality of a man in close-
fitting jeans made a refreshing change from the Paul
Smith suits, handmade shirts and indecently expensive
haircuts favoured by the men in what, until very recently, had been her everyday life.

Actually, despite the fact that it brushed his collar,
she had to admit that whoever cut Gregor McLeod's
hair knew what he—or more probably she—was doing.

'You might want to do something about this kettle,'
he called out, breaking into her idle musings.

On the other hand, in the politically correct world of
corporate management no one would have expected her
to make the tea. Not that it made a whit of difference
when it came to the crunch.

To make it to the top at Markham and Ridley, you
still had to pee standing up.

'You could do with one of those kettles that switch
themselves off,' he said, as she returned to a kitchenette
filled with steam. Not bothering to acknowledge him,
she flipped it off, dumped a tea bag in a mug and
poured on the boiling water.

It *was* supposed to switch itself off. Clearly it was
past its use-by date. Along with the rest of the store.
The whole street.

'I think Maggie might have other things on her
mind,' she said, as she added some milk and a pile of
sugar to the mug before placing it on the desk behind him.

'So who will be taking care of things?' He eased the glass into the opening and set to work with the putty. 'While she's in hospital.'

'Um? Oh, I've no idea,' she said, dragging her eyes away from the swift, deft movements as he pushed it in place with a broad thumb. She might have added that it wasn't his either, but had no wish to prolong the conversation. 'Maybe her son will come home and sort something out.'

'Jimmy? I doubt it. He couldn't get away fast enough.'

'You know him?'

'We went to the same school. What about you?'

'Did I go to the same school as you and Jimmy Crawford?' she asked, more as a delaying tactic than because she hadn't understood what he meant.

He laughed. 'You've got to be kidding. You have the kind of voice that goes with the panama hats, blazers and privilege of St Mary's Ladies College. Or somewhere very like it.'

And obviously, Juliet thought, if the rumours that had flown around after his disappearance were true, he would know all about that.

'I just wondered if you knew Jimmy Crawford,' he persisted.

'Oh, I see. Well, I suppose I might have seen him in the bookshop but I've never spoken to him.' He didn't look as if he believed that her motive was totally altruistic. 'I haven't lived in Melchester since I left for university.'

He shrugged. 'If you say so. It's just that I'm still trying to get my head around why you'd go to all this trouble. You could have just slipped the lock on the door and left once the ambulance had taken Maggie to hospital.'

'I'm a caring and responsible citizen,' she replied, trying not to think about her initial panicky response. That split second when she'd nearly bolted.

'Oh, right. Well, that would be it. So where have you been living? London?' She didn't give him any encouragement. He didn't need any, taking her silence for assent. 'And now you're home. What was it? Marriage break up?'

He was relentless. Another five minutes of this and he'd have her entire life history including the whole sorry story of her return home to lick her wounds.

A sharp and continuous rapping on the front door saved her. 'Actually, I think I'll get that. Since I seem to be stuck here for a while I might as well do something useful. Like sell some books. If you'll excuse me?'

She didn't wait to discover whether he did or not. She might not have much of a clue about the retail book trade, but it had to be a lot less trouble than Gregor McLeod.

Greg watched her go. The woman had class written all over her and it wasn't just the voice. She was prickly, though, and definitely on the run from something. No make-up, hair like a bird's nest, his first impression had been one of disappointment. But then she'd bent down to pick up that piece of glass and when she'd looked up at him it was as if he'd been there before.

Something about her silvery-grey eyes had been so familiar, the wisp of streaky fair hair that had worked its way free of pins, and he'd found himself on the brink of saying, 'Haven't we met somewhere before?'

Fortunately, he'd managed to stop himself. She couldn't have made her lack of interest plainer and it didn't take much imagination to work out what her response would have been to an old chestnut like that.

CHAPTER THREE

'WHAT are you doing?'

Juliet stopped struggling with the heavy table and looked around. McLeod was leaning against the nearest bookshelf watching her. He'd replaced his shirt and looked as if he might have been there for some time, which seriously irritated her for some reason.

'I'm moving this table,' she explained, as if speaking to a very small child.

His look suggested that he was considering a rerun of his 'sarcasm' comment. Obviously he thought better of it because he said, 'I'll rephrase the question. What are you doing struggling with that table—'

'Because it's in the way,' she snapped. Three times she'd had to squeeze around it to reach a book for a customer, three times she'd banged her shin. Enough was enough. It hadn't taken her ten minutes to see that the whole shop needed reorganising... 'What's the point of having books on display if no one can reach them?' she demanded.

'—when all you had to do was call me and I'd have helped,' he finished, moving to the other side of the table and gripping it in a pair of strong, capable hands. 'So, Juliet, where do you want it?'

He was facing her, arms wide, shoulders like an iron girder for heaven's sake. So...in her face. So... physical. Worse, he had a look in his eye that appeared to tempt her to take his question any way she wanted. She cleared her throat and stepped back.

'Nowhere.'

'Really?'

He put a world of meaning into that word. Mostly disbelief. She suspected that the answer he expected, the one he usually got, was 'anywhere.' She had been wrong when she'd thought she could handle his type. Gregor McLeod wasn't a 'type.' He was unique.

A long time ago she'd thought he was uniquely kind...

'Really,' she said, ignoring the fact that she was considerably warmer than she should be considering the chilly March weather and the poor heating in the shop, but nothing on earth would tempt her to take off her sweater.

Now she understood that he was just uniquely provoking...

'In that case you'd better clear the books off it first. If the legs come off I should be able to get it in the van.'

Uniquely irritating...

'The van?'

'You want it out of the way, don't you? There's a skip at the yard, I'll dump it in that.'

'You can't!'

'It's no bother.' And he did something with his mouth, one corner lifting up in something that wasn't a grin, it wasn't even a smile, but it was definitely...something. 'I'll just add it to the bill.'

A bead of sweat trickled down the back of her neck.

Uniquely sexy.

'No!' Oh, good grief. 'I mean...' She hadn't a clue what she meant. 'Forget it.' Then, 'Are you done?'

'All ready for inspection, ma'am.'

'Good. That means I can go.'

She turned her back on the table and crossed to the front door, flipped the lock, shot a bolt near the floor, then jumped as she straightened and turned to find Greg blocking her way.

'You missed one,' he said, reaching above her to slide home a bolt at the top, giving her a close-up of his broad chest and a whiff of mingled masculine scents—leather, some illusively subtle aftershave, linseed oil from the putty...

'You're quite sure about the table?' he enquired, stepping back to let her escape.

'What? Oh, yes.' She was nearly thirty years old, for heaven's sake. She did not drool. Not even Paul had reduced her to that. Had not even come close, but it was as if having once let down her guard she was now vulnerable... 'I just got carried away for a moment.' She retrieved an untidy strand of hair that had escaped the pins and tucked it behind her ear. 'It's one of the pitfalls of the job.'

'You're in furniture removals?'

She managed a smile. 'No, McLeod. I am, or least I was until very recently, in corporate management.' Although how anyone so good at 'managing' could have made quite such a pathetically bad job of her life was hard to see. Paul, unlike Gregor McLeod, hadn't even been on her list...

'Really? And that involves shifting furniture, does it?'

'It involves dealing with problems,' she said.

'And the table is a problem. Tell me, princess, if I told you I had a problem would you be overcome with an almost irresistible urge to fix it for me?'

She could not believe he'd said that.

She really could not believe that she was blushing...

'I'm afraid you're going to have to stand in line. Right now I'm the one with all the problems and until I've found a job and somewhere to live...' She stopped. That was more than he needed to know. 'What I don't need is the encumbrance of a bookshop that's going downhill fast. Just like everything else around here. What's the matter with these people? With a little imagination—and a fresh coat of paint—this area could be a real attraction.'

'Your imagination must be taking regular workouts. This area needs levelling so that we can start again from scratch.'

'You're kidding, surely? Prior's Lane is full of character. Full of history. The cathedral and castle are real magnets to visitors and this used to be the place where those people came to spend their money.'

'Not since the new shopping centre was built.'

'The new shopping centre's just a carbon copy of a dozen others all over the country. This is different.'

'It's certainly that.'

'All it needs are some decent places to eat, a bit of a face-lift and the right publicity to attract retailers back into the area. Like the Portobello Road. Or The Lanes in Brighton.'

'Isn't the antiques trade a little over-subscribed?'

'Forget antiques. There used to be lovely little shops down here. There still are a few, although you have to look for them. A good baker's, a terrific Italian delicatessen—you've already tried their products—and there's a hardware shop like something out of the nineteen-fifties. A real showpiece. You can still buy individual screws in there. Nails by weight.' She could see that he didn't get it. 'What Prior's Lane needs is the kind of shops you don't see anywhere else. There used to be a wonderful haberdasher's, and a hat shop…'

'A hat shop?'

'Well, okay, but when I was a little girl I used to stand and gaze in the window just dreaming…' Realising from his expression that she might just be getting a bit carried away, she shrugged and said, 'It's shopping as recreation.'

'Obviously it's a girl thing,' he said. Then, with the kind of grin that should be an arrestable offence, 'Although I like the sound of the loose screws.'

She considered responding with 'innuendo is very unattractive in a man' but decided that ignoring him would be infinitely wiser and simply said, 'Not that it's any of my concern, of course.'

'I can see that you haven't given it a moment's consideration.'

'It didn't need a moment. One look was all it took.' It would make an interesting project, something really worthwhile. If she didn't have more pressing problems to worry about. 'I haven't got time for more. Or to start shifting furniture about on a whim.' No matter how much it needed doing. 'And presumably Maggie likes it this way.'

'Maybe. Or maybe she just doesn't have anyone to help her shift this stuff. Maybe you'd be doing her a favour.'

'Possibly, but really it's none of my business. How much do I owe you?'

He shrugged. 'As you so rightly pointed out, it's none of your business.'

'I called you. I'll pay the bill.'

'Why don't I just send it to the landlord?'

'But I don't know who that is.'

'I do.'

'Right.' Then she frowned. 'Would he be responsible for the replacement of a broken window?'

'If he's difficult about it I'll give you a call and you can buy me that dinner you promised me.'

She ignored the little shiver of anticipation that rippled through her. She'd made enough mistakes for one year and it wasn't even Easter yet.

'I didn't promise you anything, McLeod. What about the security grille and burglar alarm?'

His eyes creased to a roguish smile. 'Ah, well, that's another story. But I'm open to negotiation.'

Refusing to rise to yet another innuendo, she said, 'Won't Mr Duke object to you moonlighting? Using his van, his old stock, for your jobs on the side?'

'Duke will never know.'

'I see.'

'Do you, Juliet?'

She saw that he was involving her in ripping off his employer. 'Maybe I'd better call him. Settle the bill direct.'

That dealt with the smile.

'Are you trying to get me into trouble? When I gave up my lunch date for you?'

'No. No of course not,' she said, totally out of her depth now and with the shoreline fast disappearing... 'I'm sure you'd prefer cash in hand for the alarm,' she said, trying to gather her wits and remember where she'd left her handbag.

'I've already told you, I don't want your money.'

She had never had so much difficulty outgunning a man's gaze, or found it quite so difficult to look away. 'That's really very generous of you,' she managed through a mouth that was suddenly bone-dry. 'I'm sure Maggie will be very grateful when I tell her.'

His smile returned. It wasn't the full-blown version, but rather more thoughtful, leaving her with the uncomfortable feeling that he knew something that she didn't. But all he said was, 'I'd better show you how this alarm works before I go.'

Go? That was it?

He turned and led the way to the office. 'Do you want to check the window?'

Apparently it was.

She picked up the cup of cold coffee she'd abandoned and took a sip to moisten her lips. 'It looks fine.' Then, belatedly, 'Thank you.'

'That sounded as if it very nearly choked you.'

'Did it? I'm sorry. Maybe I'm coming down with a cold or something. I'm really very grateful. You've done a good job.'

'Are you saying that you'd recommend me to your friends?'

Friends? She didn't have any friends. She'd been working too hard to make friends. She had colleagues, business acquaintances and a cheating ex. None of whom wanted to talk to her right now. Or possibly ever.

'Of course.'

'Just a fraction too long before you answered there, Juliet, but thanks for the effort.' He turned to the switch he'd fitted to the wall. 'This is very simple. Just turn it on when you leave. Down for on, up for off. There's a ten second delay before it wakes the dead.'

'That's it? Isn't there a code I need to know?'

'No. This isn't anything fancy, just a simple contact wire connected to the back door and window,' he said as he showed her how to set it, 'but it's loud, which is usually enough to deter the opportunist thief.' Then, 'Are you sure you don't want me to help you move that table before I leave?'

'Quite sure.'

'Okay. I'll be going, then.' He took a card from his shirt pocket and handed it to her. 'That's my mobile number in case you have any more little jobs that need doing.'

He was going? Just like that? She'd expected him to repeat the offer of dinner at the very least. He'd implied she owed him as much. But no, he climbed into the seat of that tired old van, started her up and with a casual wave was gone.

Right. Well, okay. That was good. She'd wanted him to go.

She closed the door.

Now she could leave too.

First she printed a note to inform customers that the shop would be closed temporarily and stuck it on the front door. Then, after paying for the books she'd bought, counting the money in the till and leaving a note to say exactly how much it was, she put them all in one of the shop carriers and tucked it away in the bottom of her basket under her mother's shopping. Then she picked up her flowers, flipped the alarm switch and let herself out of the rear of the shop, making sure that the door was firmly shut behind her.

Juliet put the narcissi on the bedside cabinet and leaned over the bed.

'Maggie?'

'Hello, dear,' she said, looking very small in the high hospital bed. Very fragile. 'They're pretty.'

'Mum sent them. She said to tell you that she'll play your bingo cards for you. Split the winnings.'

Maggie laughed. 'That's the way we do it. She's such a dear. And so are you. I don't know what would have happened to me if you hadn't come to find me.'

'I just did what anyone would have,' she said guiltily. 'How are you feeling?'

'Very stupid. I keep telling them that there's nothing wrong with me except for a few bruises. I just came over a bit dizzy, that's all.'

'Well, I won't disturb you for long. I'm sure that rest is the very best thing for you right now, but I thought you might be worrying about the shop.'

'No, dear, you said you'd take care of it and I believed you.'

A trusting soul, too...

'I've had the window fixed and locked everything up.' There didn't seem to be much point in bothering her with the details of the rudimentary burglar alarm fixed up by McLeod.

'You have been good.'

'It was no bother and the man who dealt with it said he'd send the bill to the landlord.'

'The landlord?' She tried to laugh, but it was obviously too much effort. 'He'll be lucky. He won't even fix the things he's supposed to take care of.'

Juliet offered her water, settled her back against the pillows, then said, 'Don't worry about that for now.' She'd have to go down to Duke's Yard and see if she could find McLeod. Sort things out. 'What I really need to know, Maggie, is what you want me to do with the money from the till. I've got it safe, but it should be in the bank. And there's the key, too. What do you want me to do with that?'

'Money? There was only the float.'

'Well, I stayed while the window was fixed and people kept coming in. And of course I bought two books, so there's quite a bit...'

Realising that Maggie's eyes had drifted shut and that she was talking to herself, Juliet picked up the flowers and went in search of something to put them in.

On her return she was waylaid by a nurse. 'Did you call earlier? Mrs Crawford's relative?'

Oh, good grief. She'd forgotten all about her little white lie.

'Yes,' she said. 'And then again, no. I'm Juliet Howard and I did call, but I'm not actually related. I knew you wouldn't tell me how she was unless I said I was family.'

'So who are you?'

'No one. Well, obviously I'm *someone*...' She stopped. 'My mother knows her. I found Mrs Crawford this morning and called the ambulance.' She gave an apologetic little shrug. 'Sorry.'

The nurse frowned. 'So you're a neighbour, then?'

'Not even that, I'm afraid. Just a customer in her bookshop. Is there a problem?'

'Nothing that a relative—or a neighbour—couldn't have fixed. The thing is Maggie could do with some personal things. Nightwear, toothbrush?' she offered hopefully.

'No one else has been to see her? Didn't she ask you to call anyone?'

'She told us her son is overseas and she refused to give us a contact number. Said there was nothing he could do so there was no point in worrying him.'

McLeod had more or less suggested he wouldn't

want to be bothered. She had told the truth when she'd said she didn't remember Jimmy Crawford. It was possible that he was older than McLeod, of course.

'I don't suppose you have any idea how to get hold of him?'

'I'm afraid not and Mrs Crawford is right about one thing, he can't do anything about the toothbrush.' Then, because there didn't seem anything else she could say, 'Actually I've got her keys. I'll ask her if she'd like me to fetch some things for her if that will help.' And hopefully find a neighbour willing to take over. 'How long is she likely to be in hospital?'

'It's difficult to say. Mrs Crawford said she had a dizzy spell. We'll be running some tests, but it's likely she's had a mild stroke.'

'In that case someone will have to get hold of her son and let him know what's happened so that he can make whatever arrangements are needed.'

Quite early in this sentence Juliet realised that no matter how concerned she was about Maggie the staff nurse had caught sight of something behind her that was claiming her whole attention and she turned to see what it was.

Not a what. A who.

'McLeod.'

The jeans had gone. He was wearing a pair of good looking casual trousers, a soft shirt and a fine suede blouson jacket. And he was carrying a bunch of flowers that made the narcissi she was holding look totally inadequate although she was too busy being grateful that she'd taken the trouble to wash her hair, coat her washed-out complexion with a little make-up, to care about that.

It wasn't that she'd anticipated seeing McLeod

again, but there had been the possibility that she'd run into someone else from school. Someone who might remember her. At least that was what she'd told herself...

Her mother hadn't said a word, but had looked well pleased as she'd handed over the keys to the rust-bucket she laughingly called her car to save Juliet a three-bus journey to the hospital.

'It's nice to see you, too, princess.'

'Please don't call me that.'

He shrugged. 'How's Maggie doing?'

'As well as can be expected.' Then, seeing the nurse's hopeful expression, 'Sorry, he's not Maggie's son. He's just the odd job man.' She turned to him. 'Why are you here? Oh, no, don't tell me. Maggie said that the landlord would refuse to pay for the glass.'

His eyes momentarily darkened and she felt the heat from a flash of pure anger. 'I'm sure that when you've had time to think about it, you'll wish you hadn't said that.'

She didn't need time to think, she was already sorry. But there was just something about all that unbridled testosterone that irritated the life out of her. But at least she was feeling something. Even irritation was better than the low grade depression she'd been enduring for the last few weeks.

'She's through here, McLeod,' she said, turning abruptly on her heel and leading the way to the small bay with half a dozen or so beds where Maggie was being cared for. She didn't look back to see if he was following. It wasn't necessary. The whiplash ripple of turning heads as she passed assured her that he was on her heels.

'She's asleep,' McLeod said.

'Please don't feel you have to linger if you have a more pressing appointment,' she said, putting the vase she was holding on the locker. 'I'll be happy to tell her you called when she wakes up.'

'I'm in no hurry.' He smiled at a young nurse and handed her his flowers. 'Can you find a vase for these, sweetheart?' The girl blushed and took them without a murmur.

'Why didn't you ask her for a cup of tea, top of the milk, two sugars?' Juliet asked. 'While you'd got the smile turned on.'

'You remembered.' And he regarded her from beneath heavy lids for a moment, his look so thoughtful that her own cheeks began to heat a little. Then, apparently satisfied, he turned to Maggie, whose eyes were now open.

'Hello, Maggie,' he said, dropping a kiss on her forehead. 'I heard you'd been in the wars.'

'Gregor…' She smiled. 'How lovely to see you. Are you visiting someone?'

'Just you. I heard what happened and came to see if there's anything you need. Do you want me to try and get hold of Jimmy? Let him know what's happened?'

'Oh, no, you mustn't bother him. He's far too busy to come running home every five minutes,' she said.

'Someone has to take care of the shop,' he pointed out. 'Juliet's been doing a fine job—'

'Maggie,' Juliet interjected. The last thing Maggie Crawford needed just now was to be bothered about the shop. 'You're going to need some things. I'll be happy to go and fetch them for you.' Then, 'Or if you've a friend or neighbour you'd prefer me to call?'

'Oh, heavens, that would be difficult. There aren't many neighbours now. People used to live above the shops but no one wants to do that anymore. It's all offices these days.'

'Offices?' Juliet glanced at McLeod, hoping for some explanation.

'Maggie lives above the shop,' he said. 'I assumed you knew.'

She stared at him. Was that why he'd fixed the alarm? Of course it was. Damn it, now she *did* feel bad.

'No,' she said. 'I wish you'd mentioned it. I could have brought some of her things with me.' And once again she wished she'd kept her mouth shut. Getting ratty with him wouldn't help. None of this was his fault. 'Never mind, I can go and fetch them now. Is there anything in particular you want, Maggie?'

'That's very sweet of you, dear, but there's no need to worry yourself. I keep telling them I'm not stopping. If they'd just bring me my clothes—'

'You can't go home just yet, Maggie,' Juliet said gently. 'You'll have to stay just for a while, while they run some tests.'

'Oh, no, that's quite impossible. As Gregor said, there's no one to look after the shop.'

Juliet glared at him. Thoughtless, stupid man. Worrying the poor woman. Who could say when she'd be fit to work in the shop. On her feet all day.

He smiled back in a manner that suggested she was about to deeply regret that 'odd job man' remark, then said, 'As I was saying, Juliet did a very good job today. In fact she was all ready to start moving furniture around—'

'Not before time. I keep meaning to get someone in to move that table. I'm always banging my leg against it.'

'Then she's your girl. She's in management—'

'Not retail management—'

'And, by good luck, she's looking for a job, too. Why don't you ask her to take over until you're back on your feet?' he continued as if she hadn't spoken.

'Oh, I couldn't bother her,' Maggie said, saving her the embarrassment of explaining how impossible it would be.

'It wouldn't be a bother, would it, Juliet?' McLeod persisted. 'You've a lot in common, you know. She's very keen on restoring the Prior's Lane area to the way it used to be.'

'Oh, don't get me started on that,' Maggie began.

'No, really, I'd love to help, but—'

'And there's the top floor flat. It is still empty, isn't it? Juliet's looking for somewhere to live, too.'

'Are you? Well, I suppose staying with your mother is a little restricting for both of you. It'll need a good seeing to, I'm afraid. All those stairs are a bit much for me these days.'

'McLeod!' Juliet snapped. 'Maggie, take no notice of him. The last thing you want is someone you scarcely know running your shop or moving in up-stairs.'

'Oh, I've known you all your life, Juliet. And your mother is the kind of woman I'd trust with my life. But it's not just the shop. I have to go home because of Archie.'

'Archie?'

'Archie?' McLeod echoed.

Who or what was Archie?

'He can't be left on his own, poor thing,' Maggie said, oblivious of their horrified exchange of glances over her bed as she struggled with whatever drugs she'd been given to stay awake. 'He pines so when he's on his own. And of course he has to be fed.' Then, 'You did find his food, didn't you, dear?'

Well, that wiped the smile off McLeod's face. Not that she had anything to look pleased about.

'Of course she did,' McLeod said quickly before she could own up. Then, 'Will you be all right for a while if I run Juliet into the city to collect some things for you?'

'I don't need a lift.' Especially not on the back of that motorbike. 'I've got transport.' After a fashion. The BMW that had gone with the job had, well, gone— with the job. 'Is there anything special you need, Maggie? Or will you leave it to me?'

'Don't you bother about it, dear. I told you, I'm going home—' She made an effort to sit up, just to show them that she meant it, before subsiding weakly against the pillows. 'Well, maybe you're right. I should stay in for tonight. But only if you'll promise to stay with Archie.'

'Of course she will,' McLeod promised for her. 'It won't be a problem, will it, Juliet?'

'No problem,' she repeated after the barest hesitation. 'We'll talk about it when I get back, but right now I need to go and fetch your things. McLeod will stay and keep you company until I get back.' She glanced up at him pointedly. 'That's if you don't have a dinner date?'

He smiled lazily, not in the least fazed by her barely concealed hostility. 'Well, now. That rather depends on you, Juliet.'

CHAPTER FOUR

GREG allowed her to escape, if only to enjoy the grand-stand view of her departing rear encased in a pair of softly draped trousers as she walked away as quickly as she could—short, that was, of breaking into a run and betraying the fact that Archie not only hadn't been fed, his very existence was news to her.

Whatever she'd been doing in London, he decided, she must have been very good at it if the quality of her clothes was anything to judge by. Which begged the question, What was she doing back in Melchester? Fine city though it undoubtedly was, and expanding fast, London seemed the obvious milieu for anyone in 'corporate management.'

'What a lovely girl,' Maggie said as he turned back to her.

'Exactly what I was thinking.'

'I doubt that, Gregor.' Her laughter subsided into a fit of coughing, then, letting her eyes drift close, 'Why don't you go with her? The city is no place for a young woman on her own at night.'

'Exactly what I was thinking,' he repeated. But she was already asleep. He stopped at the nurses' station to explain that they'd be returning later and then walked out into the car park.

The first thing he saw was an aged car with the bonnet up and the unmistakable figure of Juliet Howard bent over it. He'd have recognised that pretty *derrière* anywhere. 'You know I'd have put you down as the owner of something sensible and smart,' he said.

'Really?' She straightened. 'Well, you can't always be right.'

'True. But I can always be useful.'

'Prove it by making this start.'

'The only useful thing I'm prepared to do for this pathetic excuse for a car is call a scrapyard and have them put it out of its misery.'

'No good with engines, huh?'

'That tactic won't work with me, princess. I've got nothing to prove, especially when my trusty steed is eagerly waiting to gallop off with a damsel in distress.'

'You're offering to lend me your motorbike?'

'Not in this lifetime. What I'm offering is to drive you to the shop. In my car.'

'I'm sorry, McLeod, but my mother told me never to take lifts from strange men.'

'I'm not strange.'

'That's a matter of—'

'I'm not even a stranger.'

She started, as if he'd touched a nerve, and the feeling that he knew her intensified. Had she worked in one of his offices? But, if that were the case, she'd have recognised him too. And if she had? Why wouldn't she say so?

'McLeod—'

Anticipating further argument, he brushed his concerns aside—he could run a check later—and said, 'Before you say another word I should warn you that you'll have to wait twenty minutes for a taxi, minimum, and although I suspect you think it might be worth it, just give a thought to poor, starving Archie.'

'I'm trying very hard not to,' she declared, slamming

down the bonnet lid before she extracted her bag from the car and locked it. 'I promise you, nothing else would persuade me to accept a lift from you.'

'Take my word for it,' he said, 'nothing else would persuade me to offer you one.'

And finally he got a smile. 'I guess I deserved that.'

'Without a doubt, but we'll discuss your unaccountably hostile attitude towards me some other time,' he said, not returning the smile or suggesting that over dinner would be a good time. She would be expecting that and have her snappy little refusal all ready for him. It was time to move the game up a gear and stop being so predictable. 'Come on, I'm parked over there.'

She paused as he approached the long, low bulk of his immaculate midnight-blue vintage E-type Jaguar and opened the door for her.

'This is yours?' she asked, the barest catch in her throat. She definitely hadn't expected something like that.

'Odd job men get good tips,' he said.

'No...'

First the smile and now she was just a little bit flustered. As flustered as when she'd turned from locking the shop door and had found herself standing too close to him. There was something very appealing about a self-possessed woman losing her cool. The extra touch of colour in her cheeks emphasized by the lighting that leached all other colour from her skin...

'I just meant...' Her gesture indicated that she wasn't quite sure what she'd meant. He could take a pretty good guess.

'You meant, have I borrowed it? And, more importantly, did I get the owner's permission before I did?'

'Yes...' Then, 'No! I'm sorry. I don't know what I meant.'

And an apology. The full set. He was finally getting somewhere.

'It's a beautiful car, McLeod,' she said, sliding into the seat with the easy grace of a woman who knew how to climb into low sports cars. Rear end first, then legs. 'She's a real classic.'

'She is,' he agreed. Then, referring to the car, 'And you can rest assured that I have the owner's full permission to use it.'

She looked up at him. 'It's yours, isn't it?'

'Every last cog and piston,' he assured her, closing the door on her before sliding behind the wheel and starting her up.

He never got tired of the soft, throaty roar of the engine, the way people turned to look as he passed them in the street. He could have driven any car he wanted, the fastest sports car, any of those symbols of wealth that poor-boys-made-good drove to demonstrate to the world that they'd arrived. He'd got half a dozen to choose from in the underground garage beneath his Thames-side apartment in London, at the rambling cottage he'd just bought in a village within driving distance of Melchester. But this forty-year-old beauty was his favourite.

It never failed to make women—even cool, totally self-possessed women like Juliet Howard—catch their breath.

'Did you restore it yourself, McLeod?' Juliet asked, carefully polite, her breath apparently well under control as he took the ring road, heading for the old part of the city. 'The Jaguar?'

He could do polite, but he wasn't letting her get

away with that. 'Surely you aren't suggesting that a simple odd job man could restore a car like this to museum condition?'

'I don't believe I ever suggested that you were simple. And I'm aware that in the pursuit of their passions people are capable of extraordinary things.'

'Restoring cars is not my passion.' He stopped for traffic lights and glanced at her. 'I've got more interesting things to do lying on my back than getting covered with grease.'

If he'd anticipated some sparky response to such blatant innuendo he would have been disappointed. She said nothing and, with her profile backlit by street lighting, it was impossible to see her expression. Instead she lifted her hand and tucked back a smooth wing of silky hair behind her ear with slender fingers in a gesture that was nervous, he decided, rather than flirtatious.

It gave him the uneasy feeling that her confidence was all on the surface. That there was fragility beneath the poise and the self-assurance was nothing more than a surface mask—well polished, but very thin. It brought out all his most protective feelings and he found himself wishing he'd offered her reassurance rather than provocation. Wanting to reach for her hand and say, *Don't worry. It'll be all right. I'll make it all right.*

Madness.

Neil was right. Women like Juliet Howard had always caused him trouble. He was a lot safer with women he understood. Straightforward women who knew exactly what he was offering, knew he'd give them a good time, mutually enjoyable sex and absolutely no commitment.

But when had 'safe' ever appealed to him?

He pulled smoothly away from the traffic lights—this was not a woman to be impressed with boy-racer starts—and said, 'Look, I wasn't trying to manipulate you back there.'

She glanced at him. 'I'm sorry?'

He didn't believe that 'sorry.' She was far too quick not to know exactly what he was talking about. But then he was being a touch economical with the truth himself. Not about the flat. Although it would be perfect. For him. If she moved in he'd be able to take all the time in the world playing her at this game they'd embarked upon. And he'd have the perfect get out clause the minute he felt his independence was threatened...

But he played along anyway.

'About the flat,' he said. 'It'll probably need decorating—I seem to remember a lot of black and red and I don't suppose Maggie's changed it since Jimmy left. But there's plenty of room up there. You said you needed a job and somewhere to live. This would mean all your problems were solved at a single stroke.'

'The only problem I have is you,' she snapped.

'And Archie,' he reminded her.

She raised her hands in a helpless gesture. 'All right. And Archie. But that's just temporary. I can't possibly take responsibility for Maggie. Or the shop. Who knows how long it will be before she's back on her feet? The nurse said it was probably a mild stroke. It's possible she'll have another.'

'And if someone doesn't take over straight away, someone competent, the shop will close, you know that, don't you?'

'You're the second person to say that to me today.'

'Well, you know that I'm not just saying it, then. And obviously it won't be a long-term thing. She's a bit confused at the moment, but once she realises what's going on Maggie will take steps to organise someone permanent.'

'She'll need home help too. She won't be able to live alone in a first floor flat. Suppose she has another stroke. It could be thirty-six hours before anyone even missed her.'

'Given that kind of ammunition, Jimmy'll have her in a nursing home quicker than you can say the words.'

'You seem to know him pretty well.'

'Well enough. He takes after his father. The only person he's interested in is himself.' Then, catching her curious look, 'Maggie was very good to me when I was in trouble and needed someone. Buy me dinner and I'll tell you all about it.'

'I've got a better idea. Why don't you move into the flat above the shop yourself? That way you'll be on hand if she needs anything.'

'I'm not the one who needs somewhere to live,' he pointed out. 'And I've got a job.'

'What as? A snake oil salesman?'

'Excuse me?'

'You're giving it the hard sell, McLeod.'

'Me? What have I got to gain?' He struggled to keep his grin under control. *Snake oil salesman.* If Neil had heard that he'd never live it down… 'I'm simply trying to help everyone. It's your decision, Juliet. Take a look before you decide.' He'd been easing the long car through the narrow lanes near the cathedral and finally pulled up at the rear of the shop. 'But first we have to take care of Archie. What do you reckon he is?' he asked as she unlocked the door and turned off the alarm.

'Your friend Jimmy didn't have a taste for exotic pets, did he?' she asked.

'You really don't want to know the answer to that one.' She raised her eyebrows as if to suggest he needed to grow up. Obviously she thought he was kidding. 'How long do wolf spiders live, do you think?' he asked. 'And pythons?'

'Oh, please…' she muttered contemptuously. But she couldn't quite repress a shiver.

'Yes, well, it was a long time ago. Archie's probably nothing more interesting than a neurotic budgie.'

'Probably. Even so, I'm beginning to wish we'd owned up and asked Maggie who or what Archie is before we left the hospital,' she said, bending down to peer under the desk.

'We? You're the one she left in charge. I'm just here out of the goodness of my heart,' he said. 'And I don't think you're likely to find Archie there, Juliet, or we'd have seen him this morning.'

'Not me,' she replied. 'I wasn't looking.' Then, straightening, 'But you're right, there's nothing here.'

'Time to brave the unknown, then.'

'You are such a comfort.'

He extended his hand. 'Take my hand if you're scared.'

'Keep your hands to yourself, McLeod,' she said, opening the door that led upstairs, then leaping back with a shriek as something soft and furry flew out of the dark.

And suddenly she wasn't so keen to reject him. No objections now as he caught her, held her close.

She really was trembling and he knew he should feel

bad about teasing her, but holding her felt much too good to indulge in sham regret.

Her hair, scented faintly with shampoo, brushed against his cheek, the soft cowl neck of her sweater had the unmistakable touch of cashmere and her body, even through her jacket, was enticingly curvy. With considerable difficulty he kept his hands still, resisting the hot rush of desire that urged him to go for it, pull her closer, turn her in his arms and kiss her. His treacherous body said, *It'll be all right. She wants it as much as you do.*

Maybe she did. But he wasn't taking any chances. When he kissed her he wanted to be able to see her face. Wanted to know that she'd die if she had to wait another moment.

'It's okay,' he said, easing back a little. It didn't come out quite as authoritatively as he'd intended and he was forced to clear his throat before he said again, 'It's okay, Juliet. It's just a cat.'

'I knew that…'

Juliet gave a little shudder. She hadn't believed in the spider or the snake, but just the thought had been enough to lift the hairs on the back of her neck and although she pulled free it was with considerable reluctance. After the kind of day she'd had the temptation to lean into a pair of strong arms, no matter how annoying the man they belonged to might be, was almost overwhelming.

But she'd fallen for that once when she'd been trapped in a lift just long enough to feel claustrophobic. Had that all been planned, too? No matter, it had been her mistake, why she was back at square one, starting again from scratch, and she'd always made a virtue of learning from her mistakes.

Never repeating them.

And, stepping away from the invitation in his too husky voice, she stooped to stroke the cat, murmuring softly to reassure him that she wasn't a threat.

'I was really hoping Archie would be a budgie,' she said, her smile rueful as she picked him up. He was comfortingly large and cuddly, ginger with a white bib and paws. A storybook cat. She had longed for one just like him when she was little. 'I could have taken a budgie home with me.'

'You couldn't take a cat?'

'My mother has already got me back home disturbing her peace. I suspect a cat might just be one lodger too many. Even supposing she wasn't allergic to them. Come on, Archie,' she said. 'Let's go and find you something to eat.'

He butted her chin with his head, purring loudly.

McLeod dealt with the litter tray while she fed Archie and filled his water bowl.

'Thanks for doing that,' she said.

'It's what an odd job man's for.'

'Oh, look, I'm really sorry I said that. It's just—'

'I know. You've had a rotten day.'

'I've had worse,' she admitted. 'In fact this one could have been a great deal worse without your help.'

'Before you start getting too nice, I think I should make it clear that Archie is not coming home with me.'

'You can't say your mother's allergic,' she replied. 'I've already bagged that excuse.'

'I haven't seen my mother for years, so that isn't the problem.'

'Oh…' She bit off the expletive. 'I'm really sorry.'

'It was her choice. I've learned to live with it. But I

still can't take Archie off your hands. I'll be away to-morrow night.'

'Oh. That's convenient.' Then, 'Holiday or work?' As if it mattered. Before he could answer, she said, 'Sorry, none of my business. I'd better go and put together some things for Maggie.'

'Actually, it's my daughter's eighteenth birthday. Her stepfather is throwing her a party.'

'Oh.' *He had an eighteen-year-old daughter?* She did a rapid calculation and realised that she must have been born just before he disappeared from school... 'I didn't know. I'm sorry.' Then, 'Not about the daughter. About the stepfather.'

'It's okay. We're all being very civilised. He's allowing me to pay for it.' Then, 'While you're looking around for Maggie's stuff, don't forget to check out the sofa.'

Still trying to get her head around the fact that Gregor McLeod had a grown-up daughter, she said, 'The sofa?'

'You promised that you'd be stopping. Remember?'

There were so many questions she wanted to ask him. Had he been married? How long had it lasted? What was his daughter's name? If she'd been honest, owned up to recognising him, she could have done that...

'Actually,' she managed, looking away, 'I believe you were the one making free with the promises.'

But she had gone along with it. She looked down at Archie who, having made short work of the food she'd given him, was now stropping himself against her legs, purring desperately, wanting to be picked up and cuddled.

He was missing Maggie, undoubtedly. And was

probably afraid he was going to be left for more long hours by himself.

'I don't seem to have much choice,' she said, giving Archie a reassuring hug. 'But it's just for tonight. I'll sort out something long-term tomorrow.'

Sorting out stuff was what she did best, after all. How difficult could it be to organise care for one book-shop, cat included? It wasn't as if she had something more interesting, exciting, important to do. The alter-native was sinking back into the pit of self-pity.

'That's the spirit and, just to show that I'm not leav-ing you to cope unaided, I'll do my best to sort out your car for you when we get back to the hospital.'

To suggest that McLeod looked smug would have been a gross understatement but, despite an almost overwhelming urge to kick his shins, she just about managed to restrain herself. Men offering to fix her mother's car were pretty thin on the ground. Non-existent, unless they were being paid an exorbitant hourly rate for the job, actually. Nevertheless she re-fused to appear entirely helpless when faced with the complexities of the internal combustion engine.

'It's probably just the spark plugs,' she assured him. 'It usually is. I had my emery board out to give them a quick clean when you turned up and did your Sir Galahad act.'

'I think you're confusing me with some other knight errant,' he said, 'but if I need to borrow it I'll let you know.' He took a mobile phone from his pocket. 'I have to make a phone call. Can you manage the pack-ing?'

'First lunch, now dinner? Whatever you do, don't tell her the truth, McLeod, she'll never believe it,' she warned, firmly quelling the ridiculous sense of disappointment, annoyance that while he was flirting outrageously with her some other poor woman was waiting for him to turn up.

The wretch just grinned at her and, leaving him to it, she went in search of Maggie's bedroom.

What else had she expected? He was the youth who'd picked her up, dusted her off, called her 'princess,' when all the time he was making out with some sixth form 'queen' from St Mary's.

She'd been a kid. He'd been kind when she'd been hurt, but apart from that he'd scarcely been aware of her existence. The fact that she'd adored him, that her heart had nearly broken when he'd just disappeared off the face of the earth, was not his fault.

She was hurt now, a little subconscious voice prompted. Why not let him pick her up again, dust her off...

Because she was all grown up, that was why. Big enough to fight her own battles. And maybe it was time she started doing just that.

Then, pushing him firmly out of her mind, she looked around. Despite its city centre location, the flat had all the chintzy cosiness of a country cottage. Smoke-darkened oak beams added to the illusion, although the original open fire in the sitting room had been replaced with a gas fire that looked pretty much like the real thing.

Staying overnight certainly wouldn't be any kind of a hardship. In fact, babysitting a bookshop—cat included—suddenly sounded a very attractive proposition. It didn't exactly fit her job description. It was, however, useful if unpaid employment that would help out someone who'd been kind to her when she was a little girl. Whom her mother considered, if not exactly a close friend, then a cherished acquaintance.

She might even bring her laptop and start a major overhaul of that fine work, Juliet Howard's Master Plan for Her Life.

Then, as she opened bedroom drawers, found nighties, slippers, a dressing gown, and piled them into a small holdall, she decided that she might think about reorganising the shop too.

It would be a small project but at least there wouldn't be a glass ceiling keeping her firmly in her place.

She moved on to the bathroom, found a bathrobe, towels in the airing cupboard. Tossed in a tin of talc.

'A penny for them?'

She jumped at the sound of McLeod's voice, turning to see him standing in the doorway watching her as she scanned the bathroom shelves, checking for anything vital that she'd missed.

'A penny?'

'For your thoughts. You were miles away.'

'I wasn't questioning what you meant, it was your grasp—or lack of it—of inflation that I was querying.'

'If you don't want to tell me, princess, you just have to say so.'

'Actually, I was simply trying to decide what I'd want if I was in hospital.'

'To go home.'

She smiled. 'That sounds heartfelt.'

'I had my appendix removed when I was six.' He straightened. 'Come on. You can always take in anything else she needs tomorrow.'

'Yes, I suppose so.'

He held out his hand for the bag she'd packed. She

was quite capable of carrying it herself, but saying so would provoke another of those edgy little exchanges so she surrendered it without a murmur and gave Archie—who'd stuck to her heels like glue all the time she'd been packing Maggie's bits and pieces—a big cuddle and assured him she'd be back very soon before shutting him inside the flat. She didn't want a repeat of that furry rush out of the dark. Not when she was on her own.

At the hospital McLeod dropped her off at the entrance and, taking her car keys, left her to settle Maggie. When she returned half an hour later the car engine was running. He turned it off, climbed out. 'Try it,' he said.

It fired first time. 'Good grief. You're a genius.'

He made a slight bow, then said, 'It will have to be a very good dinner.'

'Sorry?'

'The one you owe me.'

'Actually, this one is down to my mother, McLeod. It's her car.'

'I did it for you, Juliet. I'll look to you to settle the account.'

'Oh, look—'

'Don't panic. I've cancelled the table reservation for tonight.'

'Excuse me?'

'What else did you have planned? Once you'd done your duty visiting the sick?'

So that was why he'd turned up. He knew she'd be there...

She firmly quashed any inclination to be flattered by his persistence and said, 'My plan was to scour the local paper in the hope of finding a flat I can afford to rent,' she lied.

He grinned. 'Well, that's sorted, so we can concentrate on food. By the time you've picked up what you need it'll be too late for anything but a carry-out. What's your preference? Since you're paying. Chinese, Indian? Or there's a very good Thai—'

'Back off, McLeod. I never agreed to buy you dinner and even if I had done...'

No, no, no! Now she'd given him an opening.

'Yes?' he prompted, taking it.

'I prefer to do the asking. Decide the where. And when.'

'I think we both know that if I leave it to you it will be the first cold day in hell.'

It would if she'd any sense... 'Half the pleasure is in the anticipation,' she said sweetly.

'Half? I think someone's been short-changing you, princess.'

'Really? I was referring to good food, fine wine and excellent company. Maybe you had something else in mind?' And finally she had something to smile about. 'Fast food, perhaps?'

'Ouch.'

'Anytime.'

'Okay. I'm prepared to spend a little time anticipating good food, fine wine and excellent company. Let's say until Saturday. After that be prepared to turn up and pay at my convenience.' And he didn't give her an opportunity to tell him what to do with his convenience but carried straight on with, 'In the meantime you're going to need a lift back to Maggie's. Unless your mother is prepared to offer you her car on a full-time basis?'

'No, she needs it for work but you don't have to play chauffeur. I was planning on calling a taxi.'

He didn't argue, just said, 'Please—let's not have that conversation again. I'll follow you.' And he closed her car door before climbing into the Jaguar.

By the time he'd started it she was out of the car park. She wasn't exactly keen on returning to the dark access lane behind the shop on her own, but she certainly wasn't going to allow McLeod to believe she was incapable of managing without him. Not that she imagined she'd have to and, sure enough, the next time she looked in her mirror she could see the Jaguar following at a safe distance.

It was ridiculous to feel irritated by his certainty that, sooner or later, she'd fall for his undoubted charm. She'd be the first to admit that he had every reason for his self-confidence; he had no way of knowing that she'd just had a booster shot against manipulative men with blue eyes and charming smiles and was now totally immune.

She just wished he'd go and find someone more appreciative to flirt with. Someone who didn't object to being called 'princess.' The girl he'd stood up at lunchtime, for instance.

'I won't be long,' she said when he pulled up outside what had once been quite a grand old house but had long ago been divided into small flats.

For one awful moment she'd thought he was going to insist on seeing her to the front door and that she'd be faced with the prospect of explaining who he was. She might be rising thirty, but her mother would take one look and put two and two together and believe she knew exactly why she'd taken so much trouble with her hair and make-up for the first time since she'd lost her job: she'd feel like a teenager bringing home the school bad boy. Not that she ever had. She wasn't *that* stupid. Her mother had drilled into her the necessity of having a proper education, a good career. All she'd ever brought home from school was homework and more homework.

Until now.

'I just need to explain where I'll be,' she said discouragingly. 'And pack an overnight bag. I'll be ten minutes tops.'

'Take your time. I'll stay here.'

On second thought, as the archetypal bad boy, he'd probably spent a lifetime avoiding tight-lipped mothers, she realised.

He needn't have worried. Her mother hadn't returned from her weekly game of bingo and she quickly dashed off a note explaining where she was, leaving it with the car keys.

He was leaning against the Jaguar when she emerged, talking into his cellphone. He straightened when he saw her and, flipping it shut, slipped it into his pocket.

'Is she getting impatient?' she asked.

'He,' McLeod replied, taking her laptop and the overnight bag and opening the door for her. 'It was work.'

'Oh.' Then, 'It's rather late for that, isn't it?'

'You know how it is, Juliet.' His smile was slow, starting at one corner of his mouth and working its way up until his whole face joined in. 'An odd job man's work is never done.'

She got into the car without saying another word. He was still grinning when he slid in beside her. Let him laugh. She'd already apologised. She wasn't about to grovel.

'Did you decide what you'd like to eat?' He glanced at her. 'You *are* hungry?'

She was starving. For the first time in weeks she could have eaten the proverbial horse but she wasn't about to admit it. Maggie would undoubtedly have a can of baked beans that she could heat up and have on toast.

'Thanks all the same, but I think I'll just hold myself in anticipation until Saturday.'

'Saturday?'

'That was the deadline you set, wasn't it? Shall we say eight o'clock at the Ferryside?'

'The Ferryside?'

'Is there an echo in here?'

'Can you afford the Ferryside?' he asked.

Probably not, but it had been worth it just to see him momentarily lost for words.

'I told you, McLeod. I don't do cheap dates.'

CHAPTER FIVE

GREG forced himself to resist all kinds of urges, not least of them the urge to kiss Juliet Howard and hang the consequences. He'd learned a lot over the years, especially patience, how to wait for what he wanted, and he'd wanted her from the moment he'd picked up the telephone and her cool, touch-me-not voice had jarred loose something primitive in him.

It was the same impulse to reach beyond his grasp that had got him into so much trouble as a youth. The same drive that had pushed him to take so many risks and, finally, come home ready to stamp his mark on a city that had once disowned him.

But time and experience had tempered his impetuosity. Had taught him that hurling himself against a closed drawbridge brought him nothing but pain. That with sufficient patience—and enough money to oil the hinges—almost any door would open to him.

Almost.

All his instincts warned him that Juliet Howard would need a subtler approach. In fact they were suggesting, quite strongly, that he'd be wise to take those 'hands off' warnings she'd been flashing him all day very seriously indeed. It was probably no bad thing that he'd be spending a couple of days at the other end of the country where temptation couldn't get the better of his best intentions because, for the first time in as long as he could remember, he felt like tugging against the restraints, kicking over the traces and letting the consequences go hang.

He climbed out of the car before he could forget himself—he'd have opened her door too and helped her to her feet, but she didn't give him the chance—and set her bag inside the back door of the shop once she'd unlocked it, remaining outside, well out of harm's way.

'Are you going to be all right here on your own?' he asked.

'It's rather late to be getting a conscience about pushing me into it, don't you think? Or was that a prelude to the suggestion that you should come upstairs to check for burglars under the bed?'

'No, you're safe,' he said, raising a grin. It didn't come easily, but he felt certain she'd expect it. 'I checked earlier. Make sure you reset the alarm before you go upstairs.'

'I won't forget. Goodnight, McLeod.'

As she moved to close the door he blocked it with his shoulder. There was a moment of resistance, her eyes widening slightly as he took her arm and pushed back her sleeve. Then, without taking his eyes from her face, he reached into his jacket and took out a ballpoint pen.

'Call me and tell me where you'd like me to pick you up on Saturday,' he said.

The smooth white skin of her forearm was warm and faintly scented with vanilla, a temptation to the senses. It took every bit of will-power to stick to his original purpose and use it as a blank sheet on which to write his telephone number.

'I already have your number.'

'You do?'

Of course she did.

He'd given her his card, but this had been about more than giving her his number. It had been much more primitive than that. It had been about touching her, putting his mark on her, and the momentary still-ness before she pulled free suggested that she knew it too.

'And I was so certain you would have thrown it in the bin the minute my back was turned.'

'Why would I do that?' she asked, her silvery eyes gleaming in the reflected security lights of the phar-macy next door. 'Good odd job men are such... trea-sures.'

Her sarcasm was oddly reassuring; she was using it to keep her distance, suggesting she was fighting her-self as well as him. Which was promising.

'Thank you for the ''good,''' he said.

'Credit where it's due.' Then, 'Besides, I thought you were confident that I'd be here...' and the unspo-ken 'waiting for you' hovered between them for a mo-ment before she continued '...seduced by the top floor flat into taking care of Archie and the shop.'

He shook his head. 'I suspect that any response I make to that is only going to cause me grief. Shall we just say that I'm taking nothing for granted other than good food, good wine and excellent company?'

His reward was an unforced smile.

'Oh, that's good, McLeod. You're really good.'

For a moment he was transfixed by the fleeting glimpse of a dimple just above the corner of her mouth as a synapse connected and something stirred in his memory.

Why couldn't he remember?

'McLeod?'

'Sorry, I was speechless there for a moment,' he said. 'I'm so happy you appreciate how hard I'm trying.'

'Trying,' she replied, 'is a very good word, but be sure that's all you'll be getting. And, since this is just dinner and not a date, I'll meet you at the restaurant.' Then, 'If you don't turn up, I'll just assume you've been distracted by some woman needing her stopcock fixed.'

'Damn it...' But before he could tell her that it would be no more than she deserved if he stood her up, he found himself facing a closed door. 'Trouble,' he muttered, recalling Neil's warning. 'Definitely trouble.'

But as he stepped back, looking up at the first floor, waiting for a light to reassure him that she'd made it upstairs without disaster, he discovered he couldn't do a thing about the wide grin spreading all over his face.

Of course he couldn't possibly let her have the last word...

Juliet made herself some supper, then, with Archie sitting at her feet purring loudly, she spent an hour surfing the Web, looking at recruitment sites, each of them urging her to sign up and let them find her the job of her dreams. Yes, well, she'd already signed up with the major players and they weren't beating a path to her door.

It drove home the painful fact that the job she'd always wanted, the one she'd worked for, was no longer remotely attainable.

The truth of the matter was that no job would satisfy her other than the one she'd earned with hard work, long hours and sheer dogged effort when the 'boys' were having a good time doing whatever it was that 'boys' did after work. She was forced to admit that nothing would satisfy her but the sight of Lord Markham on her doorstep admitting that he'd made a mistake. Telling her that Markham and Ridley needed *her* to implement the plan—the culmination of all her ideas, all her experience, put together over so many years as she'd slow-stepped her way up the ladder to the top—and begging her to come back on her own terms.

Now that *was* stupid.

The first rule of management was that no one was indispensable but she called up the file anyway. The one that she had kept so safe, determined that no one should see it until it was finished. Except Paul. She'd been vain enough to want his opinion. His praise. Wanting to impress him with her cleverness...

Archie butted her ankle. As she bent obediently to rub his ear she saw the number that Gregor McLeod had written on her arm.

Safe? Oh, right. Inviting McLeod out to dinner had scarcely been the act of a woman hooked on safety.

But exactly where had keeping her mind on business, playing safe, got her?

She'd fallen for Paul simply because he'd appeared the very opposite of the kind of predatory male that any woman determined on a career avoided like the plague. Despite his boyish good looks, perfect grooming, he'd seemed so... She struggled for a word to describe him and all she could come up with was *harmless*. Not much of a reference for a lover. But she'd felt in control with him. He'd never pushed her, had let her set the pace. She'd thought it was because he was her temporary shadow. That he was taking care not to overstep any invisible line while they worked together. She'd liked him for that. She'd felt *safe* with him.

So safe that she'd talked through her ideas with him, flattered by his interest, calling him in the middle of the night to tell him when her opus was finished. He'd arrived twenty minutes later bearing champagne, insisting that they must celebrate.

Was that when he'd copied it, downloading it in seconds on to the little memory stick that he carried on his key ring, while she'd been fetching the glasses? She'd expected him to make a push to stay that night...and knew that she wouldn't have resisted. Instead he'd made some excuse about a family get-together that weekend, an early start.

He hadn't touched her at all, until that Judas kiss that had mussed her lipstick and delayed her just long enough to put some distance between them.

What had he done? Closed his eyes and thought of the directorship?

'Make that stupid times two, Archie,' she said.

His soft burble, somewhere between a purr and a mew, was comforting. Maybe, when she found somewhere of her own, she would visit the animal rescue centre and offer a home to some other lost soul.

'Oh, for heaven's sake, Juliet Howard,' she exclaimed. 'Stop feeling so damned sorry for yourself. You're not the first person this has happened to and you won't be the last. Get over it. Move on...'

Or at the very least *move*.

Living at home, being cared for by her mother like a needy child, was no way for an adult to behave. She was done with self-pity. And, carrying Archie with her for company, she climbed the stairs to the top floor to take a look at the flat beneath the eaves.

It had the same floor area as Maggie's flat but the living space was smaller because of the sloping ceilings. And the dark walls didn't help. McLeod had not been kidding about the black and red. Very Gothic. But it was nothing that couldn't be fixed with a few cans of paint.

Maybe, she thought, he'd fix it for her. It would cost a lot more than dinner, she was certain, even dinner at the Ferryside, and she found herself smiling at the prospect of haggling over the price.

Irritatingly full of himself the man might be, but he had reminded her how to smile…

Then, slightly shocked at the wave of pleasurable anticipation evoked by the thought, she went back downstairs, settled down on the sofa for the night and with Archie at her feet lay awake thinking about how easy it would be to turn that large, if awkwardly shaped, entrance hall into a workspace with an L-shaped desk under the sloping ceiling. Pale buttermilk walls would make it so much lighter, and there would probably be good floorboards beneath the nasty carpet…

Pure fantasy, of course. She didn't need a workspace.

But it was rather more interesting than counting sheep.

And a lot more effective in distracting her from the undoubted pleasure to be obtained from getting up close and personal with McLeod. That was somewhere which, despite the very real temptation, she had no intention of going…

*   *   *

The postman woke her, ringing on the shop doorbell with a package from America that had to be signed for.

'How's Maggie? I heard she had a fall. Nothing too serious, I hope.' He handed her a pen and held out the clipboard for her to sign. 'Are you taking care of things while she's in hospital?'

'It looks that way,' she said as she handed him back his pen before taking the package and a pile of letters and closing the door.

She sifted through the mail as she walked to the back of the shop, leaving the package—which, according to the shipping label, contained books—on the desk. There were a couple of bills but the rest of the mail looked personal, so she put it to one side to take to the hospital with her before heading back upstairs to take a shower.

She'd just reached the half-landing when there was another knock, this time on the back door. A quick glance out of the small window confirmed that it was the Duke's Yard van standing in the lane at the rear of the shop.

The hippity-hop leap that her heart gave was a dead giveaway; she might, in theory, know that Gregor McLeod was not the kind of man a sensible woman would ever get involved with, but reality had a way of creeping up and catching you on the blind side. 'Bad boys' didn't get their reputations for nothing. It took more than a pair of blue eyes and a smile that could reduce the knees of the most determinedly 'good girls' to jelly if they had a mind. Men like Gregor McLeod exuded an almost irresistible air of danger. A Pied Piper magnetism.

Maybe it had been her good fortune that none of them had ever so much as noticed her.

Or maybe not.

'Safe' could get to be a habit.

'Couldn't stay away, hmm?' she asked as she slipped the locks, then felt a total idiot when she opened the door to discover that it wasn't McLeod standing on the step, but a middle-aged man she'd never set eyes on before. He was wearing painting overalls, carrying a tool-box, and had the confident smile of someone who was sure that his arrival was good news.

'Miss Howard?'

She nodded.

'Dave Potter. Mac sent me.'

Crushing a disappointment so intense that she could almost taste it, she said, 'Did he leave something behind yesterday?'

'Sorry?'

'When he fixed the window?'

Startled out of his smile, Dave Potter glanced up, then said, 'Mac fixed your window?'

Concerned that his good deed might have got him into trouble, she said, 'In his lunchtime. Maggie Crawford is an old friend.'

'Oh, right.' Then, 'I don't know anything about that, he just asked me to redecorate the top flat. He said it was urgent. I've got some colour cards so that you can choose the paint,' he said, handing her a large envelope. 'Or if you'd rather have wallpaper Mac said to pick out whatever you want and leave the rest to me.'

Paint? Wallpaper…

'No rush,' he went on when she didn't reply. 'I've got plenty to do making good and preparing surfaces before we get to the good stuff. Do you want to give me the key to the outside entrance?' he prompted, presumably taking her goldfish impression for wordless appreciation. 'That way I won't have to disturb you with my comings and goings.'

Any number of responses to this question flickered through her brain, each one more scathing than its predecessor, but this poor man was innocent and didn't deserve any of them.

There was only one person she wanted to talk to and by a stroke of luck his number was faintly printed on her arm despite her best efforts to remove it. But then there had only been cold water last night.

'Can you give me a minute, Mr Potter?' she said as she reached for the phone and dialled.

She didn't give the wretch a chance to speak. 'McLeod,' she declared furiously the minute they were connected. 'I have to tell you that you are without doubt the most—'

A voicemail prompt cut in and she stared furiously at the phone for a moment as it invited her to leave a message, unsure whether to bang it, or her head, against the nearest wall.

'Mac's on his way to Scotland,' Dave said kindly, 'so he'll probably have his phone switched off, but he said to tell you not to worry about paying me. He'll put it on the bill.'

'He said *what?*'

'Maybe I misunderstood him,' he said, backing off as she turned to glare at him.

'No. No, I'm sorry. It's not your fault.' She lifted a hand to push back her hair, then, realising that it was shaking, tucked it under her arm. 'Scotland?' she repeated.

'Some family do, I think. All kilts and bagpipes.' Then, 'I'll, um, get on, shall I?'

Kilts and bagpipes?

Why was she surprised? He might not have a Scottish accent, had certainly been brought up in Melchester, but with a name like Gregor McLeod he clearly had deep roots in the Highlands...

Replacing the telephone on the cradle with great care, she took a deep breath and then said, 'Wait here. I'll get the key.'

If he wanted to splash out on redecorating the flat for Maggie to rent out that was entirely his business, whatever hopes he might harbour to the contrary. But since she'd spent half the night thinking about colour schemes, there was no reason why he shouldn't have the benefit of her advice.

She fetched the key and then quickly marked rooms to colours on the shade cards so thoughtfully provided.

'You might want to take up the revolting carpet in the hall too. A rug will look much better once the floor's been sanded and polished,' she said, handing them back.

Well, it would.

'That was unexpectedly painless,' Dave said, clearly impressed by her ability to make a decision without a single dither. 'That part usually takes longer than the work.' Then, 'What about the rest of the flat? Do you want the floors stripped everywhere?'

'I don't want anything, Mr Potter. This has nothing to do with me,' she informed him, ignoring all that middle-of-the-night planning. Deciding what furniture she'd throw out. What she'd keep and where to put it.

That had been all so much pie in the sky.

The flat came with strings and she refused to be manipulated by Gregor McLeod. She might be out of a job, but it was a temporary blip on the 'master plan.'

She wasn't going to run a bookshop. The minute she found someone to take over, she was out of here.

She certainly wasn't going to hold Maggie to her offer of the flat in return for a simple good turn.

Then, 'Actually, bare wood would be a bit noisy, don't you think? With someone living below. Every time you dropped something it would sound as if the ceiling was coming in.' She'd once had an upstairs neighbour with stripped floors and she knew what she was talking about. 'The rest of the carpet isn't bad. It just needs cleaning.' She gave a little shrug, attempting to distance herself from any decision. 'Probably.'

Dave just said, 'Yes, Miss Howard.'

She had the uncomfortable feeling that he was taking whatever she said as an order and, having a belated attack of guilt, said, 'You'd better clear it with Mr McLeod first. It might be rather expensive.'

For a moment he looked as if he might be about to say something, but in the end left it at, 'Yes, Miss Howard.'

'I'll bring you a cup of tea as soon as I've sorted myself out.' And she went downstairs, found the switch for the water heater and put the kettle on to boil.

Her mother was her next visitor, ringing the bell and banging on the shop door until she went downstairs and opened it.

'Hello, Mum,' she said, not particularly surprised to see her, although she'd thought she'd have left it until lunchtime. 'Won't you be late for work? Second time this week.'

'Second time in twenty years,' she corrected, 'but I phoned to say I wouldn't be in until ten. I just wanted to make sure that you were okay. Are you going to take care of the shop while Maggie's in hospital?'

'It's just temporary but she was fretting about it. And her cat. Not that I know the first thing about running a bookshop.'

Her mother shrugged. 'It isn't rocket science,' she said. 'How is Maggie?'

'Mild stroke, they think. They're doing tests. I suspect at some point she's going to have to rethink living here on her own. Maybe even let the shop go.'

'Maybe, but she'll do better if she thinks she got something to come back to. I'll pop up and see her this evening. We had a little win at bingo last night, that'll cheer her up.' Then, 'Have you had breakfast?'

'No. I thought I'd pop over to the bakery as soon as I get a minute.'

'You put the kettle on, I'll go a fetch a couple of Danish.' She took a book from the new titles table and turned it over to check the jacket before looking around. 'You'd never know it from outside, but this is a great bookshop. Maggie always stocks crime books you can't get anywhere else, but it could do with bringing up to date. Most of them serve coffee these days, don't they? And snacks. But there's not much point in doing it up, I suppose. Not now it's all going to come down.'

'Come down? What are you talking about?'

'This part of the city. It's all very run-down now.'

'But it's the historic heart of Melchester. Surely it's listed? Protected? Where did you hear that?'

Her mother shrugged. 'Someone mentioned it at bingo last night. She heard from someone who knows a girl who worked as a temp in the planning department that it's going to be included in the new development plan.'

'Oh, right, just Chinese whispers. You had me worried there for a minute. Can you bring an extra pastry? There's a decorator working upstairs on the flat and I'm sure he'll enjoy one with a cup of tea.'

'Flat?'

'Maggie has offered me the top floor flat. It's rather nice, at least it will be once it's decorated. If I was going to stay in Melchester. I'd invite you upstairs to look around but Archie will have you sneezing all morning.'

'Archie?'

'Large, ginger and neutered.'

'That's a pity. Men are a bit like bicycles. You take a tumble, you need to get back on as quickly as possible before you lose your confidence.'

Slightly shocked, Juliet said, 'I thought that was horses.'

'Horses, bicycles…what's the difference? It's all just transport.'

'I haven't noticed any inclination on your part to take a trip. Was my father such a turn-off?'

'Your father…' She stopped. 'I'll go and get that Danish.'

That was two words more than her mother could usually be coaxed into and Juliet let it go. 'I could do with a loaf of bread too. And could you get some decent ground coffee and milk from the deli? Hold on, I'll give you some money.'

'Don't worry about that. You can pay me later. Tell me, this flat, is it tied to the job?'

'There isn't a job. I'm just helping out in an emer-

An Important Message from the Editors

Dear Reader,

If you'd enjoy reading romance novels with larger print that's easier on your eyes, let us send you TWO FREE HARLEQUIN ROMANCE® NOVELS in our LARGER-PRINT EDITION. These books are complete and unabridged, but the type is set about 25% bigger to make it easier to read. Look inside for an actual-size sample.

By the way, you'll also get a surprise gift with your two free books!

Pam Powers

Peel off Seal and Place Inside...

THE RIGHT WOMAN

she'd thought she was fine. It took Daniel's words and Brooke's question to make her realize she was far from a full recovery.

She'd made a start with her sister's help and she intended to go forward now. Sarah felt as if she'd been living in a darkened room and some-one had suddenly opened a door, letting in the fresh air and sunshine. She could feel its warmth slowly seeping into the coldest part of her. The feeling was liberating. She realized it was only a small step and she had a long way to go, but she was ready to face life again with Serena and her family behind her.

All too soon, they were saying goodbye and Sarah experienced a moment of sadness for all the years she and Serena had missed. But they d each other now and that's what ed.
She held asy c

Printed in the U.S.A.
Publisher acknowledges the copyright holder of the excerpt from this individual work as follows:
THE RIGHT WOMAN Copyright © 2004 by Linda Warren. All rights reserved.
® and TM are trademarks owned and used by the trademark owner and/or its licensee.

YOURS FREE!

You'll get a great mystery gift with your two free larger-print books!

The Harlequin Reader Service™ — Here's How It Works:

gency, but if I've outworn my welcome you just have to say.'

The shop door opened. 'Are you open? I heard Maggie was in hospital, but I hoped to collect a book.'

'Come in,' Juliet said, ignoring her mother's grin as she left for the bakery. 'Let's see if we can find it for you.'

She had a flurry of customers who'd heard about the accident and were anxious to collect their orders. It took time to reassure them that the shop wasn't closing—at least not in the immediate future—and she still hadn't made it to the kitchen to put on the kettle by the time her mother returned.

'Don't worry, I'll get a cup at work,' she said, placing a carrier on the desk. 'Is there anything you need from home?'

'You don't have to run around after me, Mum.'

'You're going to be very tied on your own here.'

'That's true. I'd hoped to get up to see Maggie this afternoon, get some things settled. I'd be a lot happier if she'd let me get in touch with her son so that he can take responsibility for the business. But I suppose it'll have to wait until this evening.'

'What you need is a capable girl to help out. School broke up for Easter at the weekend and one of the women at work has a sixth former who might be interested in earning a few pounds. She's a nice girl. Reliable. Shall I ask her to come and see you?'

She scarcely hesitated. Maggie was getting her for free, after all. 'Please. The sooner the better.'

'Right. And I'll come and cover for you at lunchtime if you like. You can borrow my car to run up to the hospital.'

'You know you are a really terrific mother. I don't tell you that often enough.'

'Yes, well, just be kind to the poor old dear. She started first time for me this morning.'

'Did she?'

Her memory supplied an instant playback of McLeod demonstrating this trick. The self-satisfied pleased-with-himself smile men were so good at. The one that said, *Don't you think I deserve a great big…*

'Well, excellent!' she declared. 'Let's hope the old girl's still in a good mood at lunchtime.'

Her mother's quizzical look suggested she'd gone slightly over the top in her effort to shut him out.

'Are you all right, Juliet? You look a bit flushed.'

'Fine,' she declared, grateful to her mobile phone for ringing and giving her an opportunity to cut short the conversation. 'Absolutely great. I should be there and back in under an hour, traffic permitting,' she said, waiting until her mother had gone before flipping open the phone.

'Juliet Howard.'

'Hello, princess.'

McLeod. Why on earth hadn't she checked to see who was calling before she'd answered? Given herself time to catch her breath…

'I had a missed call and thought it might be you.'

'Think again.'

He tutted. Just how annoying was that? The arrogance of the man, assuming it was her. Implying that she was lying.

Why would she lie?

Why *had* she lied…?

'So, how are you?' he asked, breaking into the confused babble in her head. 'Did you manage to get any sleep last night?'

Sleep?

Breathe, breathe, she told herself as her brain scrambled to formulate a reply. Something sufficiently distant, cool enough to indicate that she hadn't spent one second of the night awake and thinking about him.

'Sleep?' she repeated, playing for time.

'You know, you lie down, close your eyes, and if you're lucky the next thing you know it's morning. You were supposed to be doing it on Maggie's sofa. So how was it? Were you warm enough?'

'Oh, *sleep.* Yes, I was fine, thanks. Archie made a great hot water bottle.'

'I'd have made a better one.'

There was no answer to that—or at least not one that she was prepared to contemplate—so she said, 'I do hope you're not using your phone while you're driving, McLeod. Even ''hands off,'' it's terribly dangerous.'

CHAPTER SIX

THERE was nothing in Gregor McLeod's expression to betray the fact that he'd just had one of those 'light-bulb' moments—the flashes of insight that had made him so successful.

Safety.

Despite her apparent strength, her in-your-face, I'm-my-own-woman attitude, Juliet Howard—whether she was aware of it or not—was hooked on safety.

'Has Dave started on the flat?' he asked, making no effort to reassure her despite the fact that he was doing nothing more dangerous than sitting in the rear of the Rolls transporting him from the airfield; it wasn't his personal taste in transport, but it did such a good job of irritating his daughter's maternal grandparents that he was prepared to suffer.

Besides, if Juliet was worrying about him, it meant she was thinking about him. Since he couldn't get her out of his mind it seemed eminently fair that she should be similarly burdened.

'He's been at it since just after eight o'clock,' she replied. 'I'm sure Maggie will be very grateful.'

'I'm not doing it for Maggie,' he said. 'But then, unless you're not nearly as smart as I took you for, you already know that.'

'You think I'm smart?' Her ironic turn of phrase prevented that from sounding less like a plea for a compliment than an invitation to offer a put-down.

'Either that,' he said, happy to oblige, 'or so wilfully

pigheaded that you'll turn it down rather than risk being further in my debt.'

'Paint away, Gregor McLeod, if it pleases you. I owe you nothing.'

'Is that right? Then why are you taking me out to dinner on Saturday?'

There was a sharp intake of outraged breath before she said, 'Oh, go have a Highland fling, McLeod.'

And then he was listening to the dialling tone.

'Damn...'

'Is the bird with the posh voice giving you a hard time?' Neil enquired without looking up from the papers he appeared to be engrossed in.

'You could do with an update on politically incorrect labels for women, Neil, although I doubt that even in the dark ages of your youth Juliet would ever have been described as a ''bird.'''

Far from it. He might not have been overwhelmed by his first impression of her, but he was always ready to admit a mistake. His reward was her appearance at the hospital where, from the top of her glossy dark blonde hair to the tips of her designer shoes she'd carried the unmistakable aura of a successful career woman. He'd known enough of them to recognize the real thing when he saw it. So just what was she doing, out of work and with sufficient time on her hands to help out in a bookshop that was past its sell-by date?

Realising that Neil had looked up, was evidently waiting for something more, he said, 'She's an educated, elegant woman.'

'Then you really are in trouble. Don't say I didn't warn you.'

Just a touch too smugly, Greg thought, as he tossed the phone down beside him on the soft leather upholstery and picked up the architect's impression of the revamped river frontage that he'd been perusing when he'd been overcome with the need to hear her voice again.

That was one of the drawbacks of employing someone who'd known you since you were in nappies. They just had no respect...

'I'll bear that in mind when she's buying me dinner at the Ferryside on Saturday night,' he replied.

'She's buying *you* dinner?'

Well, that dealt with the smugness...

'You should pay closer attention when you eavesdrop.'

Neil shrugged. 'If it was a private conversation you wanted, you should have waited until we reached the hotel.' Then, 'You're not really going to let her pay, are you?'

'This is the twenty-first century, Neil. It's an equal opportunities dating world out there.'

And, having allowed himself a momentary smile of anticipation, he studied the mixture of conversions and new buildings that would front on to the marina development around the old dock. It wasn't, he discovered, quite enough to distract him from the thought of partnering Juliet in any kind of a 'fling.' Scottish country dancing had never been high on his list of enjoyable pastimes but suddenly he could see the attraction of the boisterous, body-clashing rush of an eightsome reel. The charge in having the waist of a flushed beauty beneath his hand as he whirled her around.

And he wished she was with him instead of his cynical right hand man.

But the city father's decision to announce the development area ahead of schedule meant he'd had to bring Neil along with him so that they could work around Chloe's party and he forced himself to concentrate. 'Mark Hilliard has done a good job. I don't see too many problems.'

'For the fee he's charging he should have the city lay down the red carpet for you.'

He allowed himself the smallest smile. 'That, Neil, is the general idea.'

'Well, don't count your chickens. Once your scheme becomes general knowledge there'll be objections from action groups dedicated to propping up every decrepit pile of old bricks in the country.'

'Pity none of them were taking an interest when Duke was letting the Prior's Lane area fall into disrepair even while he was hiking up the rents.'

'Talking of the blot on your bright new landscape, what are you planning to do with it?'

'The City would love us if we gave them some more parking spaces.'

Neil pulled a face. 'You could pave over half of Melchester and there still wouldn't be enough of those. They should be working on reducing the need for people to use their cars to come into the city.'

'Yes, well, Hilliard's having a look at how he can include it in the scheme. I'm seeing him on Friday afternoon.'

Juliet, still feeling a little shaky, went through to the little kitchen at the back of the shop and set about making a pot of coffee, tearing into the package of books that had arrived while she was waiting for the kettle to boil.

She couldn't believe she'd been so stupid. What on earth had she been thinking of, inviting McLeod to dinner at the most romantic restaurant in the county? Possibly in the entire country…

She looked at the cover of the book she was holding—a breathless and well-endowed beauty clasped in the embrace of a masterful Highlander wearing only a kilt and a plaid tossed over his naked shoulder—and dropped it on the desk as if burned.

A difficult customer proved a welcome distraction and by the time she got around to unpacking the remainder of the books she was calm enough to remember to hunt down the list of books that had been ordered and put some of them aside for the readers' group. It appeared to be good business and she wondered where they got together to discuss the books they'd been reading.

And suddenly the sofas and armchairs made sense.

Taking advantage of a quiet spell, she buckled down to work, going through the paperwork to see how the shop ran. Automatically making notes of what sold, bringing the cash in over the counter. What stayed on the shelves for months. Puzzling over the high postage costs. Letting her mind drift as she realised just how easy it would be to convert the rear of the shop into a proper lounge area where the buyers could stay to browse while they indulged in the high profit items of coffee and cake.

Was there a crime readers' discussion group? Surely, if there had been, her mother would have been a member.

If Maggie had been a client, paying good money for her expertise, she'd advise starting one, making a virtue of the fact that she concentrated on romance and crime. Shout it out loud by giving the place a makeover and turn it into the kind of specialist bookshop which fans of those genres would go out of their way to visit.

Dave's time would be much more valuably spent down here repainting the walls, brightening the place up. Or perhaps McLeod might be persuaded to put in some time for a good cause...

Her drifting thoughts were brought back into line by the arrival of Saffy, the student despatched by her mother. She had a nose stud, too much make-up and a miniskirt that displayed a yard of leg—just an average seventeen-year-old, in other words.

'My Mum said you needed some help,' she said.

'I do.' And, having laid down the ground rules and established the terms of engagement, Juliet—having banished the thought of having her rearrange the window display so that she could attract passing males as shockingly unPC—set about teaching her how the till worked.

'How're you doing, Maggie?'

'I'll be all right once they stop sticking needles in me and taking blood for tests. That nurse is worse than Dracula.'

'Well, you sound a lot better,' Juliet said, putting a carton of orange juice on the locker.

'I'll survive. How are you coping? Who's looking after the shop?'

'My mother's standing in so that I could come and see you. She'll call in herself this evening. I've taken on a girl, too, just temporarily in the school holidays. I hope you don't mind.'

'You do whatever you have to. I don't know what came over me asking you to step into the breach this way. But I'm very glad you did.'

'Blame Gregor McLeod, he put the idea in your head. He could see how worried you were. And it's fine, honestly. We curled up on your sofa and were cosy as anything.'

'You and Gregor?' Maggie enquired, with just the suspicion of a twinkle in her eye.

'Me and Archie,' she said firmly. 'I've brought your post—at least I've brought the personal stuff. The bills can wait a few days.'

'Better bring them with the cheque-book next time you come,' Maggie said, apparently resigned to staying put for the present. 'And these aren't personal letters— they're orders for books.'

'Orders? You sell by post? Is that usual?'

'Probably not, but I've been doing it for years. There was an American woman living locally who couldn't get books by her favourite authors and she asked me if there was any way I could order them for her. When she moved away she continued to order by post and it just grew from there. She told her friends about me and how great the service was and before I knew it people were writing and phoning from all over the place. Even Americans wanting books by English authors. Some people don't trust the Internet.' She handed back the envelopes. 'Can you deal with them?' she asked, leaning back against the pillows, clearly tired by the effort of talking. 'You'll find the special padded envelopes I use in the cupboard under the stairs.'

That explained the postage, then.

'Maggie, do you remember saying that you'd let me move things around? Make some changes in the shop?'

Maggie frowned, then said, 'Was it something to do with that wretched table?'

'Well, yes, but I was thinking of doing a little more

than that.' And she quickly laid out her ideas. 'I don't want to rush you into anything. Just think about it. We can talk about it in a day or two.'

'No, you're right. I've let things slip terribly. Maybe I am getting past it.'

'You're nothing of the sort. But you could do with some proper help, I think. You'll have the rent of the flat coming in to boost your income, so I'm sure you can cope with the cost of a temporary student.'

'What about you? I can't expect you to work for nothing.'

'It's okay. It's in the nature of a holiday for me.'

'It's not what I'd call a holiday.'

Juliet grinned. 'Well, maybe it's something of a busman's holiday,' she agreed, 'but I think it's doing me rather more good than lying on a beach somewhere.'

'Well, if you say so. But you'll need some money to pay this girl. You'd better ask the nurse for the phone trolley on your way out. I'll get my accountant to come in and see you.'

'Right.' Then, 'Oh, by the way, Gregor McLeod has sent someone to paint the upstairs flat.'

'Dear boy. He was a bit wild, you know, when he was young. Got himself into a lot of bother over a girl. But he's good at heart.' Then she smiled. 'And very easy to look at.'

'It's all right, then?' Juliet said, refusing to be drawn on whether or not she enjoyed looking at McLeod. Refusing to give in to her curiosity and ask what kind of 'bother'—the fact that he had a daughter suggested the answer. That 'girl.' 'I let the painter get started because you said yourself that it needed decorating but then afterwards I did wonder if I was doing the right thing.'

'From what I've seen of you, Juliet, I'd say you made a habit of doing the right thing, but you needn't have worried. Gregor popped in here at some unearthly hour before he flew off to Scotland to let me know what he'd done. He said he'd left you to choose whatever colours you wanted.'

'He did, but...'

But Maggie had closed her eyes. Whether she was really tired, or just wanted to avoid talking about the flat, Juliet would have been hard put to say. But it felt suspiciously like a conspiracy to her. They both wanted her to move in for their own reasons. Maggie, so that the shop remained open.

As for Gregor McLeod...

No. She wasn't even going to think about what he might want.

But he was right about one thing. The only reason she wasn't grabbing it with both hands was a pigheaded resistance to being manipulated. Or maybe she was just clinging to the pathetic hope that she'd be back in London very soon.

She had to accept that it wasn't going to happen. At least not in the short term. She'd already put her flat in the hands of an agent—well, her mother had—and she might just as well withdraw her name from the agencies she was registered with for all the good they were doing her. Give her whole energy to revitalising the bookshop. There was just one thing...

'Before I'm prepared to think about moving in, Maggie,' she said firmly, ignoring the closed eyes, 'we're going to have to discuss rent. And draw up a proper agreement to protect us both.' Getting no response, she gathered up the post and stood up. 'But don't worry, if you don't feel up to it I can always get in touch with your son and ask him to sort it out.'

'Don't you dare!' Maggie declared, her eyes open in a blink. 'He'll have me into a retirement home before I can whistle Dixie.'

'Not if I've got anything to do with it,' Juliet said. 'You're too young to put out to pasture and don't let anyone tell you otherwise. But when you're home and it won't disturb the other patients, I'd really like to hear you whistle Dixie.'

Maggie chuckled. 'I wish I could oblige. I can't even whistle a dog, but it's what my husband used to say. He lived in America for a while and I guess some of the phrases must have stuck.'

'You must miss him.'

'Not as much as I should, but then he wasn't the world's best husband. It was hard on Jimmy when he left, though. A boy needs a father.'

Girls need them too, Juliet thought.

McLeod might have been a 'bit wild' but at least he'd made the effort to keep in touch with his daughter, even though he couldn't have been more than eighteen or nineteen when she was born.

Maybe she had been a bit hard on him.

Later, as she walked up Prior's Lane on her way to the post office with a pile of padded envelopes, she found herself stopping to look along the curve of the narrow street, imagining how it would look with fresh, glossy black paintwork all picked out in gold with every shop decorated with hanging baskets of flowers.

What the area needed was some kind of traders' association, she decided. An action group to regenerate it. But those things didn't just happen. It took hard work and effort from someone who wasn't working all the hours in the day to simply survive. Someone with the know-how to seek out grants from the government, from historical groups.

She did her best to ignore the little voice in her head that chipped in with *someone like you,* but by the time she'd joined the queue in the post office she was into full list-making mode.

A meeting venue was the first requirement. Leaflets to lay out the objectives and get everyone there, with a personal follow-up call to rally the apathetic. And then, once it had become clear who was prepared to help and who was prepared to nod through anything so long as they didn't have to do anything themselves, a very small committee...

Her train of thought was abruptly interrupted by the headline on the evening paper being read by a man ahead of her in the queue.

New City Development Area Announced

There was a photograph of the abandoned warehouses by the riverside docks. A sketch plan of the area involved. Frustratingly, he'd got the paper folded so that she could only see half of it. The half she wasn't interested in.

Surely, though, the rumour that her mother had heard had been blown out of all proportion in the telling. No one could seriously be thinking of levelling the historic heart of the city and replacing it with an office block or a car park? Could they?

The minute she'd despatched the books she dashed

across to the newsagent's to buy her own copy before heading back to the bookshop. It took just one look to discover that 'they' could.

The editorial described Prior's Lane as a 'shock' inclusion in the plan and, while welcoming the regeneration of the docks, the money and jobs brought into the city by the new office complex, the proposed marina, it anticipated considerable resistance to this further erosion of the 'city's historic past.'

'You can bet on that,' Juliet said.

Saffy looked up from a book she'd picked up and begun reading. 'Sorry?'

'They will be. If some get-rich-quick developer thinks he's going to walk all over us, he can think again.' Then, realising that Saffy hadn't a clue what she was talking about, she handed her the newspaper so that she could read it for herself. 'It's scandalous.'

'Why? They're just going to knock down a lot of horrible old buildings.'

'Not just a lot of horrible old buildings. Prior's Lane is included.'

'So?' Then, realising that this wasn't quite what she'd hoped to hear, 'I mean, it's a bit of a dump, isn't it? Who'd come out here in the cold and wet when you can buy everything you want in the shopping centre? And those cobbles are a nightmare to walk on in high heels.'

'Maybe, but they're prettier than paving slabs and a lot harder wearing.' But the girl's reaction made her think. She'd assumed everyone remembered it the way she did, but maybe not. 'I suppose you've got a point. There's not a lot to bring people out of the warmth of the new shopping centre. It's a real shame. There used to be some lovely shops here,' she said, describing the way it had been when she was Saffy's age. And sounding, she realised, uncomfortably like her mother when that same new shopping centre had wiped out the old High Street.

The girl didn't look convinced. 'So, if they were such neat shops, why did they close?'

'Yes, well, that's a very good question.'

Definitely one for the agenda. And, aware of the value of striking while the problem was fresh in everyone's mind, she wrote out an invitation to a meeting which, since she didn't have time to find a proper venue, she'd hold in the bookshop. Then, once Saffy had been to the library to get photocopies made, she despatched her along the lane to deliver them.

Her mother arrived as she was shutting up shop.

'How did it go?'

'Fine,' she said as she bolted the door, stretching to reach the one at the top. 'My feet ache, my back aches...actually just about everything aches, but apart from that I've had a good day.'

'In that case you can't have seen the paper.'

'I've seen it. I've already organised a meeting for tomorrow night.'

'Good grief, you don't waste much time.'

'No. From being unemployed and unemployable yesterday, I now appear to have two major projects on hand. Revitalising the bookshop and saving Prior's Lane.'

'You've got the work. Have you got a client?'

'Someone to pay, you mean? No, but there'll be plenty of publicity in the Prior's Lane cause. If I handle it properly it will demonstrate that I'm not the gibbering wreck that my former employers are implying.'

'Good thinking. And there's no reason why the regeneration of the bookshop shouldn't do you some good too. It's the sort of thing that the *Country Chronicle* likes to feature. Combined with the fight to save Prior's Lane, you might even get some interest from the Sunday newspapers.'

It was rather lowering to discover that management skills she'd always assumed were the result of hard years of study and experience had probably been learned at her mother's knee. A woman who'd never had any kind of career. Pregnant and on her own by the time she was seventeen, she hadn't had much chance of that; she'd just had to take jobs that would pay the bills and fit around child care. All the while making very sure that her daughter had a better start than she had had. That her life wasn't messed up before it began.

Had her father been like McLeod? Young, scared, running as fast as he could from the mess he'd helped make? Except that McLeod hadn't run.

On an impulse she gave her mother a hug.

'Hey, what was that for?'

'Everything.' Then, 'Are you going to be home this evening? I'm going to need some of my stuff. My putting-on-a-front clothes among other things.'

'Come home with me now. We'll pick up some take-out on the way and I'll help you pack while you tell me what you've got planned.'

'How was the party?'

'Lavish,' Greg replied as he climbed into the car. 'Chloe's stepfather spared no expense.'

'Really?' Neil frowned. 'I thought you were footing the bill.'

'As I said, he spared no expense. Not that I begrudged a penny of it. She's all I've got and I see precious little of her.'

'Well, that'll change once she comes south to university, won't it?'

'Reality check, Neil. Unlike you, I never made it to university, but I'm sure you didn't waste too much time hanging out with your dad.' Then, 'Tell me what's been happening on the Melchester front. Did the announcement go ahead as planned?'

'It did.'

'And?'

He handed him a sheet of paper. 'I took this off the Internet this morning.'

Greg found himself gazing at a picture of Juliet Howard with Prior's Lane in the background. It looked quaint rather than tired in the spring sunshine. And he noticed that someone had placed tubs of daffodils outside the bookshop to add some colour. Nice touch.

'You know who this is?' he asked.

'Yes. It's "trouble." The girl with the chocolate voice has used it to good effect, organising the Prior's Lane traders into a pressure group before the ink was dry on Wednesday's final edition. They will not, according to the editorial, be moved.'

'No?' Greg grinned. 'Damn it, Neil, doesn't she look amazing? I love that suit. It shows exactly the right amount of leg. Just enough to make you want to see more—'

'I fail to see why you find it so amusing.'

'I'm not laughing. Frankly, I'm lost in admiration.' Then, 'Come on, you've got to be impressed. How long did it take her to organise all this?'

'You're the genius, you do the maths. The development plan was in the Wednesday evening edition of the *Chronicle*. This was in today's first edition. Friday.'

'Less than forty-eight hours.'

'And she was on local radio this morning too.'

She didn't just look amazing. She was amazing. What on earth was she doing messing around in Melchester? Why wasn't she running some corporation? He'd give her a job tomorrow. Today. If she wasn't doing such a brilliant one for him in directing the professional agitators' attention away from the main development.

'What are you going to do, Mac?'

'Nothing. At least nothing directly.' He'd already run a check through personnel and made certain that she'd never worked for him in any capacity. But clearly she'd worked for someone. 'I want you to get on to one of those executive head-hunting agencies. Tell them that we're in the market for an experienced, well-qualified woman for a senior line management post. Late twenties, early thirties. Someone with a strong organisational background. See if her name crops up.'

'And if it does?'

'Email me everything they've got. And in the meantime get someone to check and see if the radio interview is online. I'd like to hear what she had to say.'

He just wanted to hear her.

'But—' Neil shrugged. 'Okay, Mac. I'll get on to it.'

'And remind everyone in the office that if the gentlemen of the press try to corner them their only comment is "no comment." The same goes for any nice people who suddenly want to buy them a drink in the pub. I've gone to a lot of trouble to see that my name isn't linked in any way with this project but now it's in the public domain there'll be people very keen to find out who's behind Melchester Holdings.'

'What about Marty Duke? He's just sold you the freehold on land that he didn't know was going to be included in the development plan. He must be spitting feathers.'

Greg grimaced. The same thought had occurred to him. 'According to my information he was ready to leave the country the minute the bank transfer went through, no doubt with a pack of creditors at his heels. Let's hope they haven't caught him. Yet.' Then, 'Is there anything else that needs my immediate attention?'

'Nothing that I can't handle.'

'Good. In that case I'm going home to take a shower and change before I drive down for my meeting with Mark Hilliard. I'll be at the cottage all weekend if you want me, but please don't call unless it's a real emergency. I've got a date with a beautiful woman.'

'You're still planning on having dinner with Miss Howard? Now that she's—she's...'

Neil made a vague gesture, apparently unwilling, in the face of his obvious interest in her, to suggest exactly what Juliet Howard might be.

'Leader of the opposition?' he offered. 'Tell me, my friend, why would I pass on the prospect of hearing from her own lips what plans she has for thwarting my ambitions?'

Neil was clearly shocked. 'Well, yes, but it's hardly ethical, is it? Especially since she's the one paying the bill.'

'Hey, can I help it if she thinks I'm just an odd job man?'

'She's going to kill you when she finds out and you know what? I'm on her side.'

CHAPTER SEVEN

JULIET paused in the entrance of the pretty riverside restaurant to catch her breath. The day had started early, long before the shop opened for business, and the queries, phone calls and offers of help from people who'd seen the paper had come in at such a rate that she'd scarcely had time to think, let alone breathe.

Half a dozen times she'd picked up the phone to call McLeod and put off dinner, pleading pressure of work. If he'd seen the newspaper he must know how crazy her life had become.

Even if he hadn't seen the paper, he would want to check up on Dave's progress. Wouldn't he?

Every time the shop door had opened she'd looked up, half hoping, half dreading it would be him, coming to see for himself what was happening. Offering to take a rain check on dinner. Or at least letting her off the hook to the extent of suggesting she relax, put her feet up in front of the fire with a glass of wine, while he went and fetched the finest Chinese take-out that Melchester could offer.

On her, of course.

She'd been torn between a completely irrational desire to see him standing there and the desperate hope that he'd keep well away until Dave had finished in the bookshop so he could see for himself how great it was looking. Then, no matter how mad he was, he'd have to admit that she'd got her priorities right.

Finally, just mad that he hadn't even bothered to ring

and confirm their 'date,' she'd gone completely over-board and was now standing in the doorway of the Ferryside in her highest heels, with her lashes extended courtesy of the latest technology in mascara and wearing the kind of little black dress that in London had been the height of sophistication but which, on a Saturday night in the provinces suddenly felt just a little too low in the neckline, just a little too short in the skirt.

And she knew she should have made that call.

What on earth had made her pick this particular restaurant from all the hundreds there were to choose from in the area?

Because you wanted to impress him, stupid, that smug little internal voice that seemed to know all the answers offered far too readily. Demonstrate that you are a woman in control. A woman who can take decisions, follow them through…

No, no!

Okay, well, maybe just a little. But mostly it was the need to convince herself. Restore her self-confidence.

But the voice refused to shut up.

You wanted to dress to kill, it continued, to slay Gregor McLeod, to have him look at you and want you. To prove to yourself that you weren't still the pathetic little girl who'd trailed him around at break time, hoping to be noticed. Who'd walked on air for a week when he'd winked at you…

She put her hands over her ears to shut it up.

'Juliet? Are you all right?'

She jumped at the soft, gravelly voice, so close that she dropped her evening bag. McLeod stepped from the shadows beside the door, picking it up, his fingers touching hers as he handed it to her.

The dangerous thrill of excitement that rippled through her found a betraying echo in her voice. 'M-McLeod.'

'You sound surprised.'

'N-no. I didn't see you there. In fact I didn't expect you to be here yet. I came a little early to make sure...' He waited. 'Well, you know.'

'Have the maître d' take your card details to avoid any embarrassment over the bill?'

'It's how I've always handled business lunches... dinners...in the past.'

And this was business, she reminded herself. Buying him dinner at the Ferryside would cover all outstanding debts. At least until he'd seen the shop...

'And I came a little early because, since you rejected my offer of a ride, I wanted to be sure that you weren't sitting in the bar on your own.'

She swallowed, wishing she hadn't made that remark about 'business.' 'That's very thoughtful of you.'

'I'm a nice guy, Juliet.'

'Always ready to help out a damsel in distress. Kind to old ladies...' *Protective of little girls who were being bullied...* 'Tell me, do you take in stray dogs too?'

'It has been known. I even feed the birds in my garden,' he said, helping her from her coat and handing it to a hovering waiter as if it was something he'd done a hundred times. Completely at home in the quiet luxury of their surroundings. 'Is it politically acceptable these days to say that you look lovely? Since this *is* business?'

'Perfectly acceptable, thank you, McLeod. And so do you.' And it was true. He looked good enough to eat. His dark hair curled into his collar, sleek and glossy, the jacket of his suit sat across his broad shoulders as if it had been made for him, his tie was undoubtedly silk. He looked exactly *right*. Standing out, attracting attention only because he was the kind of man who would turn heads wherever he went, whatever he was wearing.

And yet…and yet… Despite the civilising clothes, he seemed, somehow, infinitely more threatening than he ever had in a pair of jeans and a leather jacket.

Then, blushing as she realised what she'd said, 'I meant you look smart. In a suit.'

There was nothing different about his grin, though. It still raised her heartbeat so that she could feel her pulse hammering in her throat.

'They won't let you in here wearing jeans.'

'No. Sorry. I hope you didn't have to buy it specially.'

'You slay me, princess.'

Well, mission accomplished, then. Easier than she'd imagined…

'You have a garden?' she enquired, firmly changing the subject.

'I sense just a hint of disbelief in your voice. You don't see me as a horny-handed son of the soil?'

There were some conversational gambits that were better avoided, she decided, offering no response other than slightly raised eyebrows.

He laughed. 'You're right, of course. A ride-on mower to keep the grass low enough so I can find the beer and a hammock slung between a couple of handily placed trees does it for me. We're over here.' And with his hand at her back he guided her in the direction of the bar.

She was not wearing enough dress.

She'd been concerned about the length of the skirt,

the neckline; she hadn't given a thought to the low cut of the back. Not that McLeod was being heavy-handed. On the contrary, his hand was barely grazing her skin; it was scarcely more than the transference of warmth raising the down on her back, cutting off all connection between her brain and her senses. Only touch was making it through; he had to be leaving scorch marks...

'Did you come in your mother's car? Juliet?'

'What?' Then, 'Sorry, it's rather warm in here.' She waved the little clutch bag she was carrying as if it were a fan. 'My mother's car?'

'That candidate for the scrapyard you were driving the other day,' he prompted. 'Or did you decide to play safe?'

Safe? This was *safe?*

'No. Yes...'

The truth was that she hadn't even asked. She felt too unsure of herself to risk the third degree on her 'date'; as far as her mother was concerned, she was tucked up in bed having an early night.

But she was beginning to sound like a complete idiot.

'That is, no,' she clarified with determined briskness. 'I didn't come in my mother's car. And yes, I decided not to risk the chance of having to fiddle with its innards and ruin my manicure. This was definitely an occasion for a taxi.'

'Well, I'm glad we've finally got that established. It means that we can have a drink while you tell me all about your plans to save the world from big bad property developers.'

'You saw the newspaper then,' she said, thankful to change the subject as he ushered her towards a secluded table. A waiter instantly appeared and began to open a bottle of champagne that was chilling nearby and she jumped even though he deftly twisted the bottle so that the cork made the most discreet of pops.

'You seem a little on edge,' McLeod said as he sat beside her. 'You're not nervous, are you?'

'Should I be?' Then, before he could answer, 'Are we celebrating something?'

'It isn't every day you appear on the front page of the *Melchester Chronicle* raising a standard to rally the troops against the onslaught of heathen developers. Definitely a champagne moment.'

'I don't think so.' She'd had it with champagne moments...

'Don't worry, this is on me,' he said, handing her a glass then clinking his own against it. 'To the heroine of the hour.'

'Oh, please. I'm just the traders' spokesman.'

'A little more than that, I suspect. I thought the daffodils were a nice touch.'

'Did you?' she said, taking just a sip of champagne before quickly putting her glass down so that he wouldn't notice how much her hands were shaking. It was a kind thought. A generous thought. He wasn't to know that it was her least favourite drink...

Daffodils, she thought. Just stick with the daffodils. They were a nice safe subject.

'Yes, well, I wanted to show Prior's Lane off at its best. Some really lush hanging baskets would have looked better, but it's the wrong time of year.'

'No, truly, I hardly recognised the place, but then the photographer did a really good job of keeping the background slightly out of focus so that the peeling paintwork didn't show.'

'It took a while to get it exactly right,' she admitted. 'Thank goodness for digital cameras.'

'And helpful newspaper photographers who respond to flattery?'

She began to relax. Even managed a smile. 'You are such a cynic, McLeod,' she said, risking another sip of her drink.

'Am I? Really?'

It was okay. After all, it wasn't the champagne that had ruined her life...

'I promise you, he was as shocked as I was to think such a historic area might disappear under twenty storeys of steel and concrete. And it was in both our interests to get a really good photograph.'

'Please don't tell me you talked him into providing the daffodils too.'

'What? Oh, no. Dave found me a couple of half barrels...' Damn! She hadn't meant to let it slip that he wasn't hard at work painting the flat. 'And I haggled with one of the market traders for a job lot of flowers. They were a bit past their best,' she added quickly, hoping he wouldn't query it. 'I got them for next to nothing. But then they're not sure where they're going to be shifted to either.'

'He's doing a good job? Dave?'

Obviously not quickly enough.

'He's been great. I meant to thank you.'

'I'm sure you would have done if we hadn't been cut off in the middle of our conversation.'

'We weren't cut—'

She stopped, took a breath—she was not doing at all well here—and caught the waiter's eye.

He stepped forward instantly, refilling their glasses

before rescuing her with, 'Are you ready to look at the menu, madam? Sir?'

'Thank you.'

'That was heartfelt, princess,' Greg said, even while admiring her diversionary tactics. Indicating that the man should leave the menus on the table—he wasn't ready to let her hide behind one of the huge leather-bound folders just yet—he continued, 'Anyone would think you hadn't eaten for a week.' Instead of doing her best to change the subject. And with good reason.

But then she had no way of knowing that Dave Potter had checked with him before allowing himself to be diverted from painting the flat. That he'd had chapter and verse on the work that was being done in the shop.

'Well, maybe not a week,' she said with a rueful smile, 'but the truth is that I've been rushed off my feet all day. I don't believe I've had more than a cup of tea since breakfast.' She paused as if to think about it. 'Actually, I don't remember having any breakfast.' Then, just to toss in a further change-the-subject conversational grenade, 'And, on the subject of political correctness, didn't I ask you not to call me "princess"? It gives the impression you can't remember my name.'

'No danger of that, Juliet.'

She was right, though, he was casual enough in the use of the standard endearments—'sweetheart,' 'darling,' 'babe'—and mostly for the reason she gave. Never 'princess,' though. That had come from somewhere deep inside his head...

'But don't wear yourself out over this,' he said, letting it go. It would come to him. 'At the end of the day you're going to walk away from Prior's Lane and the bookshop, go back to your real life.'

'My *real* life? It doesn't get much more real than this.' Then, looking around the beautiful restaurant, 'Okay, not *this*. But you know what I mean.'

'I know that if the people whose livelihoods are bound up with Prior's Lane don't care enough to fight for it, then nothing you do can save them.'

'But they do care. Most of them.' He raised his brows, suggesting she was being a touch optimistic. 'Obviously I'm not going to get too much support from the charity shops who are simply there on short leases. If the area becomes desirable again, they'll lose their sites.'

'In the cause of progress someone always loses.'

'If the place disappears under a megaton of concrete, everyone loses. They just need an outsider, someone with a fresh eye and time to organise the resistance.'

Or someone, Greg thought, who needed a cause to rekindle her enthusiasm, to restore her self-confidence, although seeing her sitting there, a picture of poise in a dress that would be responsible for an epidemic of cricked necks in the morning, it was hard to imagine what could possibly have brought her running back to Melchester with her tail between her legs. She certainly wasn't looking for another job...

'It's really hard for them,' she went on, when he didn't offer her any encouragement. 'They all work really long hours, you know.'

'Yes, I do know. I just hope they know how lucky they are to have you looking out for their interests.' And he finally picked up the menus, handing one to her.

It was her turn to stall as, clutching it against her, she said, 'Does that mean I can rely on you to help?

We've formed an action group and I've enlisted the aid of the historical society—'

'Thanks, but I've got a lot on right now.' And somehow he didn't think her 'action group' would take it at all kindly when they discovered she'd invited the enemy into their war room.

'Don't you care what happens? We know, more or less, what they're planning to do with the rest of the development site, but apparently the Priory area is a last minute addition. If you don't care about Maggie and the rest of them, try a touch of self-interest. Duke's Yard is included too, you know.'

'I saw the paper.'

'Oh, right.' She sat back, clearly disappointed that this tactic had failed. 'I thought it would affect you. What about your job?'

'I don't work there. I work for myself.'

'But I thought...' He could see what she thought. 'You answered the phone. You were driving one of their vans.'

'I bought it,' he said, leaving her to interpret his answer as she chose.

'The van?'

He was vaguely disappointed. If she'd called him he'd have owned up—had, in fact, done nothing to hide the truth—but it had just never occurred to her to see what was plainly before her eyes. You acted like an odd job man, you got treated like one...

'Among other things. You were right, Juliet. Marty Duke has gone out of business. I just happened to be there when you rang. The phone was cut off minutes after your call.'

'But what about the stuff you brought? The security grille, the alarm?'

'It would have gone into the skip. Forget about it.'

'Right,' she said, but she was frowning, clearly trying to puzzle something through that didn't quite make sense. There was hope for her yet.

'What did you think of the rest of the plan?' he asked. 'For the dock area of the city.'

'What? Oh, well, it sounds good on paper. I don't suppose it'll please everyone, but there's no point in clinging on to the past just for the sake of it.'

'No.'

She caught the wry edge in his voice and her eyes narrowed.

'I'm not a Luddite, McLeod. But there's a big difference between revitalising an area with exciting new buildings and burying the past under a multi-storey car park.'

'A multi-storey car park? Is that what's going to happen to it?'

'Well, it's just a rumour but you know how desperate the city is for more parking spaces and Prior's Lane is in exactly the right place for a new multi-storey. Right next to the shopping centre and all those new offices.'

'It looked to me as if the developer had made adequate provision for parking.'

As she shrugged the light gleamed off her creamy shoulders and it took all his concentration not to give in to the demands of his body and reach out, touch.

'Can't the planning office tell you what's happening?'

'They don't seem to have a clue. Or maybe that's just the impression they want us to have. And all the anonymous holding company that's fronting the development company is saying is "no comment."'

'Maybe you should consider picketing them,' he suggested.

'Oh, please. Me, my mother and Archie. That would really worry them.'

He began to laugh. Then, seeing that she was serious, quickly straightened his face and said, 'What you need is some sort of blocking mechanism to force them to talk to you. Maybe the history people will come up with some antique statute granting trading rights in the lane to the citizens of Melchester in perpetuity.'

'They're looking into it.'

'Good for them. In the meantime you seem to have got your hands rather full. How are you coping with the shop? I suppose you've had to forget about making changes for the time being.'

'Well…'

Juliet knew this was the moment to own up, tell him the truth. That she'd taken Dave away from painting the flat and set him to work painting the shop as fast as she and Saffy could shift books, reorganise the shelving. But it would all be so much easier when it was finished and he could see for himself that she'd done the right thing.

And even if he was angry with her, it would be too late for him to do anything about it. Other than send in the bill…

So she fudged it with, 'Maggie thinks the world of you, McLeod.'

He responded with a smile so lazy that it never reached his eyes, leaving her with the feeling that he knew exactly what she was doing. But all he said was, 'The feeling's mutual.'

'Then won't you help us? For her?'

'You don't quit, do you, princess?'

'Not when it's something this important,' she assured him, furious that he wouldn't get involved. And that he'd apparently forgotten her name again.

The casual nickname had charmed her as a little girl when she'd known no better, but obviously he used the same catch-all pet name for every girl he'd ever met. So much easier than having to make an effort. So much less trouble than getting a name wrong.

'And I hate to be the one to tell you this, McLeod, but your short term memory could do with some work. The name is Juliet.'

'And mine,' he replied, 'is Gregor. Use it and I promise you won't be able to keep me away from Prior's Lane.'

That wasn't what she'd asked him and he knew it.

'Really? You'd be prepared to spend all your free time envelope stuffing, making posters, organising petitions?' she pressed.

'Just say the word, princess,' he replied, deliberately baiting her with the meaningless endearment.

His face was shadowed in the subdued lighting, but his eyes gleamed with a touch of recklessness that made the heat rise to her cheeks as his voice, soft and low, issued a challenge to take the smart-mouthed flirting beyond words.

He only had one thing on his mind, she knew, and it wasn't Prior's Lane...

Maybe he wasn't alone.

Gregor...

She wanted to feel his name grate over her tongue. Whisper it softly, hear the sound...

'No. You're all right,' she said abruptly, hoping that the low lighting would conceal her colour. 'It wouldn't be fair to involve you. Not when you've, um, got a lot on.'

'Your decision. You can change your mind any time,' he said, his smile as slow as his voice. 'But maybe it's time we ordered. I suspect the maître d' would get seriously annoyed if you were to pass out from hunger. Very bad form.'

It was like the heat from a briefly opened oven door, she thought. That glimpse of something unexpected, the temptation to get her fingers burned.

The moment passed as quickly as it had come, but as she opened the menu Juliet knew that in laying out the possibilities, inviting her to take a gamble and put herself in his hands, their relationship had changed subtly and forever. Not because he would try and push her into something she wasn't ready for, but because he hadn't. He'd left it entirely up to her. And now every time she looked at him, called him McLeod, they would both know that she was thinking about what he'd said.

All she had to do was say the word.

Gregor...

She glanced over the top of the menu, hoping to steal a peek at him, and found herself looking straight into his clear blue eyes. It was a moment when she could so easily have abandoned all thought of food, grabbed him by the hand and simply run for the dark in a rip-your-clothes-off moment of naked passion.

And she knew why a girl could so easily have forgotten all her mother's wise words, her father's warnings and walked on the wild side.

Then he grinned, breaking the spell. 'Do you want to help me with this?' he asked as, abandoning his own menu, he moved closer and with his arm around the back of her chair, said, 'Us odd job men don't get taken out to French restaurants very often.'

She didn't believe for a minute that he was fazed by the menu, but she didn't actually care. The smooth cloth of his jacket felt good against her shoulder. His arm felt solid and protective at her back.

So what if it was an illusion? As long as she recognised it for what it was, straightforward sexual attraction between two adults with no pretence, no lies…

She shivered a little.

'Are you cold?'

He was looking at her, but suddenly she couldn't meet his gaze. 'No, it was just…' It was just as if a goose had walked on her grave. 'Well, maybe I should have worn something rather less…' The only word that came into her mind was 'revealing.'

Taking advantage of her hesitation, McLeod said, 'Less? Is that possible?'

'I think perhaps the word I was struggling for is "more" rather than "less." Something warmer.' And she managed a laugh. 'It's crazy, isn't it? Men go out for the evening properly dressed in a suit and a shirt, with a silk tie around their necks to keep out the draught. Women, on the other hand, seem to take it as some kind of challenge to wear as little as they can get away with.'

'Well, speaking for the men,' he said, bending to plant the gentlest of kisses on her shoulder, 'I think it's a really good system.'

CHAPTER EIGHT

'WARMER?' Greg asked, looking up, meeting her wide-eyed gaze as she struggled to find words to convey exactly how she was feeling, but the fact that she was finding it so difficult told him enough. 'You don't have to thank me,' he said. 'Central heating is all part of the service.'

It was cruel to tease, but it was just so easy to make her blush. Juliet Howard was such a muddle of contradictions. Cool, businesslike one moment. Floundering in confusion the next. And she was the one who'd insisted that this wasn't a date, something her dress denied with every clinging fibre, every inch of skin it left exposed.

She pressed her lips together firmly, refusing to be tempted into indiscretion and, ignoring him, gave her full attention to the menu, leaving him free to give his total attention to the way her hair slid over her elegant neck and fell forward to hide her face. The satiny skin of her back...

She glanced back, saw where his gaze had wandered and said, 'Keep up, McLeod. I want to eat tonight.'

'Yes, ma'am.'

For a while the conversation concentrated on nothing more disturbing than the merits of fish versus fowl, the remembered pleasures of good meals, sharing experience, getting to know one another. Easy, relaxing conversation. Relaxing enough, once the waiter had departed with their orders, for Juliet, back in control following that outrageous kiss, to venture into dangerous, personal territory.

'So, McLeod,' she began, 'how was your trip to Scotland? Did your daughter's party go well?'

'Very well, if your idea of a good time is a crush of people eating too much, drinking too much and dancing to music of ear-damaging loudness.'

'To be honest, it's not.'

'Nor mine.' He smiled as if they were a couple of misunderstood grown-ups, in it together. 'But Chloe appeared to have a good time, which is all I care about.'

'Such a doting father,' she said, the unexpected wobble to her voice catching her unawares. Not entirely in control, then... 'I don't suppose for one minute you have a photograph of her?'

'You wouldn't be making fun of me, would you?' he asked, reaching into his jacket pocket and taking a snapshot from his wallet.

The young woman smiling out of the photograph reminded Juliet so much of McLeod at the same age that instead of answering him she caught her breath. She had that same heavy, dark hair with a wayward inclination to curl. The same vivid blue eyes. But none of her father's dangerous edge. Or maybe the formal, girls-in-pearls portrait with its innocent smile disguised deeper feelings. She would, after all, have inherited a streak of recklessness from her father. And perhaps her mother, too.

'You are in deep trouble, McLeod,' she said, handing the photograph back.

For the first time since they'd met she saw him disconcerted. 'I am?' He looked at the photograph, clearly wondering what she'd seen in it that he'd missed.

'Unless she joins a convent she's going to leave a trail of broken hearts in her wake wherever she goes.' Then, 'Obviously she takes after her mother.'

'Her mother has red hair, green eyes and freckles,' he said.

'Freckles? I thought you were a gentleman!'

He grinned. 'Okay, not freckles. Just a sprinkle of gold fairy dust.'

'Oh, for goodness' sake,' she said, slapping down a nasty little green spike of jealousy that wanted to be told that Chloe's mother had big ginger freckles all over her face. That yearned to be told that she, too, had fairy dust... 'It must be tough for you, her living so far away.'

'Not nearly far enough for her grandparents. They did everything they could to keep me away from her. And Fiona, of course.'

'The freckly redhead?' she asked, as he stowed the photograph carefully away. 'Obviously they didn't succeed.'

'Not for want of trying. You know, it's strange. I hated them for years, Fiona's parents. Never forgave them for what they did. But then, at the party, I saw Chloe in a clinch with some loutish youth and I finally understood what they went through all those years ago. Understood that all they wanted to do was protect her from the likes of me.' He looked up, smiled. 'It would seem that it's my turn to suffer.'

'You're a parent. It goes with the territory.'

'Yes, well, I've had it easy so far. Turning up once a month with some new toy she'd asked for, never having to play the heavy at bedtime, be the bad guy over homework, is a piece of cake compared with the real work of being there.'

'I'm sorry. It must have been so hard for you,' Juliet said, reaching out instinctively to lay her hand on his arm. Knowing that there had been another man his little girl had run to when she'd fallen and hurt herself. Who had been there all the time to read her stories. Who had just been…there. 'You did what you could. More than a lot of men in your position.'

'It wasn't enough.'

'No.' It wasn't just his little girl he wanted. It was her mother.

She carefully lifted her hand away and then, punishing herself, said, 'Fiona's parents stopped you from being together? Getting married? Or is that terribly old-fashioned of me?'

'If it is then I'm with you, but the only thing we had in common was that we were both eighteen and ready to have a good time. She was in her last year at St Mary's Ladies College with a place at Oxford hers for the asking. I was just finishing my first year of sixth form at Melchester Comp. Totally different worlds. She was all glossy hair, polished vowels and panama hats.' He glanced at her. 'Well, I don't have to tell you.'

She remembered his assumption that she'd come from the same privileged background. 'No,' she said. 'You don't have to tell me.'

It had been on her 'list.' Part of her master plan for life. To be one of those confident, always smiling girls with identical uniforms so that old or new they were all the same…

'I was the kind of boy that she'd been warned about all her life.'

'Bad boys, especially ones with motorcycles, have an apparently irresistible attraction for well brought up young ladies.'

'How did you know I had a motorbike?'

'I'd have bet my shirt on it,' she said, covering her slip with what she hoped was a serene smile. 'My best silk shirt,' she added.

'Yes, well, her parents clearly believed that I was entirely responsible. If they could have, they'd have had me arrested for the despoliation of a virgin. Not that she was. Those clean-cut, blazer-wearing good boys from St Dominic's apparently considered it their duty to relieve the St Mary's girls of that particular burden as soon after their sixteenth birthdays as...' He stopped, clearly thinking he was telling her something that she already knew. 'Yes, well, at least I was bright enough not to tell them that.'

'So, if not quite a Galahad,' she said softly, 'very close.'

He glanced at her, his brows drawn together in a frown. Then, 'If one of her friends hadn't gone out of her way to tell me, I'd never have known about Chloe.'

'You weren't still seeing her?'

'I was never part of her long-term plans, just a summer fling to celebrate the end of school, fill in the time before she went to Tuscany for the summer. The morning sickness must have really messed up her holiday.'

'I'm so sorry.'

'It's okay, princess,' he said, reaching out and retrieving the hand that she'd so briefly used to offer some comfort, his thumb absently rubbing across the back of her fingers. 'I'd like you to believe that I was broken-hearted, but in all honesty it wasn't anything more than a case of juvenile lust at first sight. Careless lust at that.'

She tried to obliterate the image of two young people in too much of a hurry to make sure they were properly protected. A sudden yearning to know how it would feel to be so utterly lost in desire...

'Why didn't she tell you herself? About the baby.'

'She always maintained it was because she was afraid what her father would do to me. I suspect there was an element of self-preservation mixed in with that. She was in enough disgrace without admitting she'd been playing on the wrong side of the tracks. She wasn't noticeably overjoyed when I turned up, demanding my rights. But I wasn't going to allow her, or her family, to airbrush me from the family tree.'

'It does you credit,' she said.

'Yes, well, my parents thought I was crazy. Told me I should be grateful for being let off the hook, run not walk away. They just didn't understand, refused to help. In the end it was Maggie who found out what I had to do, helped me get a court order for a blood test to prove paternity. Then, before it could be served, there was a For Sale sign outside the house. No one home.'

'So *that's* where you went.'

'What?'

She realised that her stress was all wrong. That she'd said it as if she'd missed him.

'You went after them. To Scotland,' she said quickly.

Then, 'Oh, no. That would have been easy.' He shrugged. 'Easier. I have family in Scotland, would have had somewhere to stay at least. But Fi only moved there when she married her laird, years later. No, I finally tracked them down to Ireland, where I had to start the legal process all over again. Maybe that's when they realised that they couldn't pretend I didn't exist. That I wasn't going to conveniently disappear.'

'You dropped out of school to pursue her? Gave up your own chance of a place at university?'

He shrugged. 'Some things are more important.'

'I doubt many eighteen-year-old boys would have thought so.'

'Maybe I wasn't cut out for an academic career. Anyway, I was eventually conceded visiting rights, allowed to spend one afternoon a month with Chloe in the presence of her nanny.'

'Once a month! That's monstrous.'

'Maybe. Maybe they thought I'd lose interest, that it would be harder for Chloe if she really knew me. Anyway, when they discovered to their undoubted surprise that I wasn't totally uncivilised, that despite my working class background I bathed regularly, knew how to use a knife and fork, things got a little easier. I was even invited to Chloe's birthday parties.'

'With faces as stiff as the frosting on the cake, I'll bet.'

'Only the adult faces. Especially the time I arrived with a bouncy castle in the trailer. But the kids loved it.' He grinned briefly at the memory. 'And I'm a stubborn bastard. No matter how chilly the welcome, I just kept going back.'

'And now they don't just invite you to the parties, they let you pay for them too.' She couldn't believe how much she disliked them all, sight unseen. 'I hope the welcome is warmer.'

'To be honest, I've never been able to quite work out if the bagpipes are to welcome me or are an attempt to drive me away.' And then, when she laughed, 'Maybe there were faults on both sides, but she's my daughter and I'd give her the moon if she asked for it.'

'She's a lucky girl.'

'Yes, she is. She has a family who love her and a father who'd…' He shrugged.

Die for her, she thought, filling in the gap.

'What about Fiona?' Juliet asked. 'How does she feel about having you around?'

'I didn't see much of her. She took a gap year to cover having Chloe, before going to Oxford as planned. Then she met Angus and maybe because they wanted to make a point, or maybe it was just because Chloe was bridesmaid, her parents invited me to the wedding. Now they have three little Rob Roys of their own.'

'A happy ending for everyone except you, then.'

'I'm working on it. What about you? I know you have a mother who drives a wreck of a car. What happened to your father?'

'A good question. Unlike you, McLeod, he didn't make a virtue of his paternity.' She glanced up as the waiter approached them, for a moment planning to snatch the chance to walk away from a pain she'd never shared with anyone. 'The truth is, I've never met him.'

McLeod waited until they were seated at their table and they were alone before he asked the question that had seemed to hang in the air for the long minutes while they were settled.

'Do you want to? Meet him? Get to know him?'

'It's difficult,' she said, picking up a fork, toying with the seared scallops she'd ordered. 'He abandoned my mother. Ran away. I can understand how scared he was, but she had the courage to defy her parents, insist on keeping me even though they refused to support her.'

'Brave woman.'

'Hardly a woman. She was even younger than Fiona.

I saw how she had to struggle, how hard she had to work, not just to support me, but to give me the kind of chance that she'd been denied. I could never feel anything for him but contempt.'

'But?'

'But…' She sighed. 'There are these great gaps in my life and no one to ask. If she doesn't already, you can be sure that Chloe will one day realise just how lucky she is that you're the man you are.'

'Thank you. I have sometimes wondered if my welcome would be quite as warm if my appearance wasn't always accompanied by toys.'

'Toys?' She laughed. 'I'd take a bet than you aren't getting away with Barbie doll accessories these days.'

'Your best silk shirt would be safe with that one. This year the car wasn't made out of pink plastic.' Then, 'I thought you were hungry. This is really good.' He offered her a sliver of smoked duck. 'Try it.'

It seemed the most natural thing in the world, taking food from his fork. 'Mmm…'

She caught his eye and realised how close he was, how intimate the gesture. Paul had never been so warm, so spontaneous, but then, he'd never wanted anything from her but the contents of her laptop. He'd gone through the motions, but in comparison with Gregor McLeod he was completely wooden. Which was bad enough. It was the fact that she hadn't had the wit to realise it that really hurt.

McLeod, on the other hand, made it clear with every look, every gesture that he only wanted her.

And she found herself struggling for breath.

'It's so subtle,' she managed, easing back a little, going for thoughtful. 'What is that flavour?'

'I've no idea. But then I don't actually care beyond

the fact that it does the job. I'm not going to rush home and try to replicate this dish in my kitchen.'

'You don't cook?'

'Not unless the alternative is going hungry,' he admitted. 'What about you?'

She gave a little shrug. 'Maybe women are used to cooking for themselves.'

'Just for yourself?'

She smiled. 'The chef could teach you a thing or two about subtlety, McLeod. But yes, just for myself. I was involved with someone rather briefly. It's over now.'

'That's why you came back to Melchester?'

'Who says I ''came back''?'

'You did. You told me that you haven't lived in Melchester since you left for university. You're looking for a job, somewhere to live. *Were* looking for somewhere to live.'

'I seem to have found myself plenty of work. Not that any of it's salaried.'

'Maggie's not paying you?'

'We're at something of a stand-off on the issue of finances. She won't even discuss a proper rent, so I won't let her pay me for helping out. And her accountant is practically blowing a gasket at the changes I'm making. He seems to think Maggie should shut up shop altogether.'

'Funny way to do business.'

'Well, I can't say I took to him, but he's got a point. My mother partners her at bingo, but she hasn't seen me for years. I could be anyone. I could be robbing her blind.'

'You should have told him how much a pane of glass

in that back window is costing you, that would shut him up.'

'He'd probably have had a heart attack right there and, believe me, I've taxed my first aid skills to the limit this week. He calmed down a bit once he'd run my name by a credit agency and checked out a couple of references I gave him, but he's still not happy.'

'He's an accountant, he's not supposed to be happy. What he should be doing is making sure the shop continues to trade. Whatever it takes.'

'Maybe he thinks that it's not worth it,' she said, 'since, unless we *all* make a huge effort to protect the area it's going to be under a car park by this time next year.'

He shook his head, a wry grin lining his face. 'Nice one. I wondered how long it would be before you got back to your favourite subject. So, tell me, what are you offering the planning committee?'

'Offering?'

'You want to save your precious little street, but you must see that it can't be left as it is?'

'Oh, no. Well, obviously it needs a total make-over. A fresh coat of paint, flowers…' Even as she said it, she realised it was nowhere near enough. 'Actually, I have worked out why it became sidelined as a shopping street. Shoppers used to have to use the old car park by the station and walk up to the town centre through Prior's Lane. The new shopping centre has its own car park that delivers the shoppers right to the door. And Saffy said something interesting—'

'Saffy?'

'A student I've got working in the shop. She wanted to know why anyone would bother to go out into the rain and cold when they could get everything they wanted in the mall.'

'So? Are you saying that it should be covered in some way?'

'I haven't a clue if it's even possible. We could really do with an architect or a structural engineer on board.'

'They cost money.'

'This is a community project. We're all volunteers.' She ignored his choked response. 'And of course we'd have to interest retailers in moving back. I've been doing some research...' She ran on for a while, full of ideas. Then, realising that he hadn't said a word in ten minutes, she stopped abruptly. 'I'm sorry. You're clearly bored to tears. It's just that I've been living this since I saw the newspaper.'

'I'll admit, retail trade is not on my conversational top of the pops when I'm in a romantic restaurant with a beautiful woman, even if it is just dinner and not a date. But you're right about one thing. Getting a few potential retailers interested will do more good than all the petitions in the world.'

'You're only saying that because you're scared I'll ask you to stand outside the bookshop with a clipboard.'

'I'm not scared. You can ask me to do anything, princess. If I don't want to do it I'll say so.' Then, with a lift of one of those expressive brows, 'Is there anything you'd like me to do for you?'

She had the uncomfortable feeling that they'd stopped talking about the campaign. But he couldn't possibly know about the shop. He'd have said something. Dave would have said something...

'Order pudding?' she offered.

He glanced up and a waiter appeared at her side instantly. She stopped him before he could begin to list what was available and said, 'Please just bring me something with chocolate.'

'Nothing for me,' McLeod said. Then, when the man had gone, 'So, tell me more about this brief relationship that caused you to bolt for home.'

'It was a relationship. It was brief.' He waited. 'He was a bastard,' she elaborated. 'Worse. I was a fool.'

'Since you're looking for another job, I assume you worked together.'

'You are way too bright to be an odd job man, do you know that?' He just smiled. 'You're right, of course. I made the fatal error of dating a colleague.' She shrugged. 'When it all goes pear-shaped, someone has to leave.'

'He was your boss?'

'Not *that* bright. I was his. Or at least I thought I was. When he ripped off my ideas and leap-frogged over me into the boardroom, I'm afraid I rather lost it. Now that really was a champagne moment.'

'You threw it in his face?'

'There,' she said, sitting back with a broad gesture. 'I knew it. It's just so predictable. A total classic. Put a glass of champagne in a woman's hand. Make a total fool of her in front of all her colleagues and, yes, it's Bolly all over the Armani and a swift departure with the contents of your desk in a box under your arm and seven years of hard work down the drain. He calculated my reaction, wound me up—'

'Juliet—'

'—and I performed to order. But my really big mistake was not stopping there. One glass of champagne was understandable. Grabbing a tray and flinging the contents at the chairman, leaving him dripping with fizz and treading the remains of the broken glasses into the carpet, suggests you're heading for a nervous breakdown. Not just *persona non grata* at Markham and Ridley, but an employment risk that no one in their right mind will touch with a bargepole.'

'I'm sorry.'

'Why? It wasn't your fault.'

'I meant for ordering champagne. No wonder you looked so horrified. I assumed it was because you imagined I'd blown your entire budget before we'd even looked at the menu.'

'No...' Then, 'I was afraid that after you'd gone to so much trouble, so much expense, I might not be able to get it past my lips without gagging. But once I'd managed to get the shakes under control I actually rather enjoyed it.'

'Maybe it's like riding a bicycle. You need to get right back in there before it becomes a major problem.'

'How odd. My mother said much the same thing the other day.'

'About champagne?'

'No, about—' She shook her head, but it was way too late. He couldn't possibly have missed the meaning. 'What about you? There must have been some significant other in your life besides Fiona?'

'She wasn't significant. Life changing, but not significant. But you're right, there have been lots of girls, women. One, maybe two, that seemed important at the time, but somehow didn't manage to clear the final hurdle. Nothing recent. As you get older you get pickier, I suppose.' He smiled. 'And I always had high standards.'

She wondered if he was fooling himself. If the

mother of his child was the only person he could truly commit himself to, whether he realised it or not.

'What about the lunch date you ditched to come to my rescue?' she asked.

'I'm sorry to disillusion you, but I was planning to have lunch with someone who works with me. While Neil might appear to be a bit of an old woman at times, he does have a wife and small two children to prove otherwise.'

'Then why didn't you say so?'

As if she didn't know. How much more fun it must have been watching her tie herself up in knots...

He was saved from having to answer by the waiter arriving with an airy work of art created from spun sugar and chocolate.

'Good grief, I feel guilty even thinking about eating this,' she said, grasping any opportunity to move on, forget some of the things she'd said to him. Hope that he would too.

McLeod leaned forward, broke off an elegant filigree arch of dark chocolate and held it up to her lips. It crumbled as she tried to take it with her teeth to avoid touching him and, as she tried to catch it, her lips closed around his fingertips.

Time slowed down. Her heart, which usually went about its business without bothering her, thudded once, twice, three times against her ribs. Low in her abdomen, her womb contracted and every part of her felt soft, yielding, ready...

'There,' he said, putting his thumb to his mouth to capture a crumb she'd left, sucking it clean. 'It's easy.'

'Is it?' Her voice barely made it above a whisper. 'I've never found it so.'

And, as if answering a question she had scarcely

been aware of asking, he took her hand, holding it lightly between both of his. 'Life is too short to waste the simple pleasures, Juliet.'

Was it as simple as that? She'd spent all her life working. Pleasure had been for other people. And when she'd finally been tempted, her judgement—so lacking in practice—had completely failed her.

But she had nothing McLeod wanted other than the human warmth and pleasure of her body. Something that she knew he would give back in full measure.

A simple pleasure.

'Will you excuse me for a moment?'

He scarcely had time to do more than half rise before she'd walked swiftly across the restaurant. She left her credit card with a startled waiter.

'The bill,' she said. 'And will you please ask the receptionist to call a taxi to take us into Melchester.'

'But madam—'

'Now.' She didn't wait to see if he'd got the message but walked swiftly to the powder room, hoping that she'd find what she was looking for.

Her hands should have been shaking as she put the coins in the slot, but they were as steady as those of a heart surgeon. She really should have been embarrassed when a woman tidying her lipstick at the softly lit mirror caught her eye and smiled knowingly. Instead, as she dropped the foil packet into her bag, she smiled back.

She added an outrageous tip to the bill she signed, thanked the waiter for a wonderful evening and then dropped back into the seat opposite McLeod and picked up her spoon. 'I hope you don't mind passing on the coffee but we've got just five minutes before the taxi arrives,' she said.

'You've ordered a taxi?'

'Yes, Gregor,' she said. And looked up so that he couldn't possibly mistake what she was saying to him. 'I want you to take me home.'

CHAPTER NINE

GREG did not miss the significance of the deliberate way she'd used his given name for the first time. It seemed to purr off her tongue, soft as velvet, tugging at the hot desire he'd been doing his best to keep under control ever since she'd walked through the door of the restaurant.

He'd talked more than he had in years, telling her stuff that no one else knew, talking about the past to keep his mind from frying as he'd looked at her. This was not a date. It was just dinner. She'd dressed like that to punish him for behaving like a caveman and he wasn't offering any argument for the defence. At the end of the evening she was going to call a taxi and climb inside, leaving him with a last look at that sexy backside, those long legs, before waving him goodbye.

He'd spent the last four days with her continually on his mind. When had that happened before?

All his senses were working overtime. He didn't give a damn about the subtle taste of the food; it was the taste of her skin where he'd kissed her shoulder that was haunting him.

He could close his eyes and even listening to her talk about saving Prior's Lane—which right at this moment was his least favourite subject—was enough to make him hard. If he opened them the double whammy of seeing her soft mouth form the words made concentrating on what she was saying a tough call.

He had forced himself—he really did need to know

what she was thinking, planning—to the extent that he'd actually managed to drop in the occasional question so that he hadn't appeared a complete idiot, even while the combination of scents from her skin, her clothes, her hair had taken him close to meltdown.

Now she was sitting there, her liquid silver eyes regarding him so calmly that only her huge black irises betrayed what was going on inside her head and, with a single word, was offering him everything his overheated body craved.

But even while every cell was screaming 'Yes!' and 'Go for it!' something in his head warned him that this wasn't what she wanted. That it wasn't what he wanted, in his heart of hearts. When he buried himself in Miss Corporate Manager of the Year it would be because she was pleading with him for it, telling him she'd die if he didn't. Not because she'd coolly decided to take her mother's advice to get back on the bike before she lost her nerve and he was the lucky jerk she'd chosen for the ride.

He wanted her.

He couldn't believe how much he wanted her. But he wanted her boneless. Beyond reason. Out of control.

He refused to be just Any Other Business on the evening's agenda. She'd laid down the ground rules for this evening—dinner, not date—and now she wanted to break them. If he'd tried that he'd never have heard the last of it.

Easy to think, tougher to live with. He needed to cool down, give his body a chance to catch up with his head, and for that he had to put some distance between them.

'I won't be a moment,' he said, getting to his feet.

'Actually—'

He couldn't believe it. Was she really going to look him in the eye and tell him that he didn't need to visit the machine in the washroom because she'd already taken care of it?

As he waited hot colour streaked along her cheekbone and she shook her head. Whatever she'd been going to say, she'd clearly lost her nerve.

She wasn't quite as cool as she looked. And, as he stood on the steps of the restaurant, the chill air coming off the river the nearest thing he could manage to a cold shower, his heart lifted a beat.

When he returned she was still staring at the untouched dessert looking if not quite frozen with panic as near as made no difference. 'Shall we go?' he enquired, not bothering to sit down.

'But I haven't finished.'

'You're sweet enough,' he said, taking her arm and levering her to her feet without asking her whether she was ready to move or not. 'The taxi you ordered has arrived.'

'Has it? Won't he wait?'

She'd lost the bright flags in her cheeks, he noticed. In fact she had lost pretty much all her colour. Clearly she was having second thoughts. Back-pedalling that bicycle as hard as she knew how.

He recognised that, logically, he should have welcomed her change of heart. Just as he should have felt a whole lot safer as she wrapped her coat around her. It didn't work that way, he discovered.

With her long limbs, her pale skin, hidden away beneath ankle-length cashmere, his imagination went into overdrive as, somehow, what was veiled became infinitely more desirable.

And her sudden loss of confidence made him want

to take charge, make the decisions about where this was going. Toss her over his shoulder to carry her back to his cave and behave exactly like the caveman she thought him. All he needed was a chauffeur-driven limousine in which to carry her off...

As they emerged into the chill night he saw his car, safely dismissed and now out of reach, gliding away from the restaurant. His driver must think Gregor was mad. And as he'd handed him Juliet's cancelled credit card slip, disposed to pay the bill himself, it was obvious that the maître d' clearly thought one of them was; doubtless the size of the tip he'd received to compensate for complicating his bookwork would ensure that the man kept his opinion to himself.

He opened the taxi door so that Juliet could climb in. 'I don't want there to be any misunderstanding. When you say home,' he enquired, keeping his voice as cool, as expressionless as if he were negotiating a multi-million pound deal, 'do you mean your mother's house, or the bookshop?'

She hesitated a split second and for a moment he thought she was going to seize the escape route he'd offered her. Then, with an almost defiant lift of her chin, she said, 'The shop. I want to get an early start in the morning.'

He walked around the cab and gave the driver directions before climbing in beside her.

'Buckle up, Juliet,' he said, fastening the seat-belt that would keep a safe distance between them.

She wrapped the belt around her and drove the connection home with rather more than necessary force.

Did she imagine that he was going to make a grab for her the moment they were in the back seat? Sweep her off her feet so that she wouldn't have to listen to those second thoughts?

Tempted as he was, this was her game plan and she was going to have to call all the moves. He wasn't going to make it easy for her.

'Thanks for a great meal,' he said. 'The restaurant is lovely.'

'I'm glad you enjoyed it.'

Glad? Juliet could not believe she'd just said that. No, she couldn't believe he'd said that. She was a seething mass of conflicting desires and emotions and he was calmly saying that he'd enjoyed the meal.

'The duck was something else.'

How dare he be talking about food, *thinking* about food, when she couldn't actually remember a single thing that had passed her lips? All she could recall was the taste of chocolate. And his skin.

'You said,' was all she could manage in reply.

In a moment of bravado, of absolute certainty that she could carry this off, she'd said 'the word' and in doing so had all but offered herself to him on a plate. For dessert.

Gregor.

She was right, the word had felt good in her mouth. Soft as a Highland mist. Hard as granite. And now she was sitting beside him while the taxi sped them towards the city centre. She didn't care what he thought of the wretched duck. She just wanted his hands on her, his mouth doing unspeakable things. Her mouth...

And without warning the entire pretence that the evening was no more than a settling of debts collapsed like a house of cards.

Maybe it was the sudden shock of cold air as they'd walked from the restaurant to the car but that first I-can-do-this adrenalin rush had stalled somewhere between the chocolate and the chill of the taxi.

Or maybe it had just been his cool acceptance, almost as if he was doing her a favour. As if he didn't have to put in any effort to make her feel just a little bit special. It sent a chill through her. Did he imagine she did this regularly?

Did he have no idea how big a deal this was for her?

Damn him, he was sitting there, totally detached, looking out of the window, for Pete's sake, instead of at her. Touch me, she pleaded silently, begging him to read her thoughts. Just touch me. You're good with engines. Do something to jump-start my heart. Make it purr the way you did my mother's car.

He'd been flirting with her non-stop since she'd called Duke's number and he'd picked up the phone—and why had he done that if he was just buying a van?—but now he seemed more interested in the passing view of the river. The old warehouses.

What was the matter with him?

What was the matter with her?

She'd given him the green light, so why wasn't she wrapped in his arms right now, being kissed senseless before any niggles of doubt could set in? Wasn't that what men did?

Not Gregor McLeod, evidently, since they had enough clear air between them to allow not just a niggle but an entire phalanx of doubts to march between them.

How had she got so lucky?

In her dreams, this was the moment when he was supposed to look into her eyes and remember her, remember the day he'd truly been her knight and then...

No, even she wasn't that foolish.

She was bright enough to know that she was nothing more than a substitute for the woman he could never have. The St Mary's girl with the privileged background and the perfect vowels; his real 'princess.' She was simply a fake version, one whose mother had moulded her speech until it was indistinguishable from the real thing, assuring her that it would be worth it because she was going where the girls who mocked her would never be able to follow.

And she had been right. An ancient university, a first class degree, a career built on solid foundations. They had all been hers.

But those other girls had something else that she longed for. Men who loved them, children, the security of a proper family. All dreams that for her had somehow fallen on the 'downright impossible' side of the list because she'd never trusted anyone enough to let go of the safety rail.

But this was different. She wasn't asking for, expecting, a huge happy ever after, but just one night to fill the aching void. To hold close and cherish. Surely she was entitled to a tick beside one little dream?

Not in this life, apparently, and she said, 'So that's it, then. All debts paid.'

He glanced at her. 'Except for the coffee.'

'Coffee?'

'And the decorating. You are going to invite me in for coffee, aren't you? Show me how well Dave is doing fixing up the flat for you. I assumed that's why you rushed me out of the restaurant.'

Oh, good grief! She hadn't given a thought to the flat when she'd been whispering 'Gregor' across the table in a very bad imitation of some nineteen-thirties silver screen vamp. The flat actually looked worse than when she'd first seen it. The hall carpet ripped up. Blotches where Dave had made good the plaster. The paintwork rubbed down and undercoated...

'That was so bad mannered of me. I didn't even ask you if you wanted coffee or a brandy. I don't know what I was thinking about.'

'Don't you?'

She swallowed. At least it was dark in the rear of the taxi and this time he couldn't see her blush. Then she thought about it. 'Hold on. Weren't you the one who was in a tearing hurry, Mr "You're-sweet-enough"?'

Greg managed a careless shrug. 'The meter was running on the taxi.'

He heard her shuddering sigh.

'Are you cold?'

'I'm fine.'

She was far from fine and it required every ounce of will-power to stop himself from abandoning the seat-belt, wrapping her up in his arms and warming her to the point where spontaneous combustion was guaranteed. His only hope of behaving in a manner that ensured he'd be able to look himself in the mirror in the morning was to keep his distance. God bless whoever made back seat seat-belts compulsory.

'Maybe you should think about investing in some thermals to go with that dress.'

'There isn't room for me and thermals in here,' she pointed out, with just enough edge to let him know that she was not amused. Better, he thought. Much better.

And much worse. He was now unable to think about anything but the kind of skimpy underwear that *would* fit in there with her.

A thong. It had to be a thong. A tiny black lacy

thong snuggled up tight against her body. Right where his hand should be.

And precious little else.

'I noticed,' he said, completely unable to stop himself. 'But since you shrink-wrapped yourself in lycra presumably that was the intention. I imagine you did want every man in that restaurant leering at you?'

'Every man?' she asked. And as they passed a street light he saw that her mouth was fighting a smile.

'Nearly every man,' he corrected. 'I wouldn't be that obvious. And there was a gay couple in the corner who didn't even notice you.'

'Rubbish,' she declared. 'This is a designer dress. They watched it every step of the way across the dining room as we left and I'm telling you that it wasn't the food they were drooling over.'

So it was the fact that he could actually remember what he'd eaten that bugged her, was it? Just as well that she didn't know the only reason he remembered the duck was because he'd watched her lips closing around his fork.

'Drooling? Oh, please...' And they'd seen it from the front. He'd been following her. There wasn't going to be enough cold water in the entire world... 'But then it is what they call a "result" dress, isn't it?'

'Excuse me?'

'A follow-me-home-and...'

'It's shoes, Gregor,' she said, before he could say the words. '"Result" shoes.' And, as he glanced down at her feet, 'And if you value your life, I suggest you keep whatever you're thinking to yourself.'

'I was merely going to remark that you're wearing very pretty shoes.' Then, because looking himself in the eye in the mirror in the morning was something he'd worry about tomorrow. 'And they worked. You've got a result. You're home. And I'm right behind you.'

Before Juliet could begin to think of a reply, the taxi stopped behind the shop. And what was she so out-raged about? She had dressed to turn him on. Make him look. Make him want to touch. Damn it, she wanted to drive him so crazy that he wouldn't be able to help himself.

The driver opened the door for her and as she stepped on to the pavement she opened her bag to pay him. Gregor beat her to it and dismissed him.

'You might regret doing that, McLeod,' she said as the car eased quietly away down the narrow lane, leaving them alone in the tiny pool of light from above the door.

'I don't think so.' He held her gaze. 'Your key.'

She took it from her bag and handed it to him, a bundle of confused uncertainties, yearnings, muddled desires. If he would just touch her, put his arms around her and kiss·her, everything would be so simple, so easy. But it was as if he was waiting, almost demand-ing that she make the first move.

Gregor unlocked the door, pushed it open, flipped off the alarm, before standing back to let her in ahead of him.

Juliet was instantly assailed by the smell of fresh paint.

About to reach for the light switch, she let her hand fall and, turning back to him said, 'Gregor… I have a confession to make.'

'Tell me later,' he said, and before she could explain about Dave, about how painting the shop was so much more important than her flat, about how she had been going to tell him just as soon as she was sure he'd be reasonable about it—well, okay, as soon as it was finished—he carried her back against the wall, pinning her there with his body. 'All I want to hear from you right now is one word.'

She went rigid with shock.

No! This wasn't how it was meant to be…

'It won't wait…'

His hands were inside her coat, pushing up the hem of her dress as they slid up her thighs.

Oh…oh…

'About the flat…' she persisted.

His palms slid over the silky stockings, encountered the lacy tops of the hold-ups she was wearing and he made a small guttural sound deep in his throat that tugged at something deep within her…

Oh, yes…

'About Dave…'

His mouth grazed the neckline of her dress, leaving a moist trail over the exposed cleavage and, instead of pushing him away, demanding to know what the heck he thought he was playing at, she whimpered for more, tipping her head back against the wall in an open invitation to help himself.

'About the shop…'

She was beginning to lose track of what she was saying as her insides began to dissolve—

'The painting…'

—settling into a low ache as, encountering no obstacle, he cupped her naked rear in his hands and lifted her against him, holding her there so that she could feel his arousal.

'You talk too much, princess,' he said, his voice a little ragged as he lifted his head to look down at her.

No man she'd dated had ever bypassed the opening

moves in such an outrageously brazen, utterly sexy manner. Her mouth was full and swollen and, without thinking, she licked it to try and cool it. She wanted him to peel off her dress, wanted him on his knees…

'Gregor,' she said, his name an unmistakable plea. The only light came from the window display at the far end of the shop, yet his eyes glittered like hot stars. 'Please…'

'Tell me what you want, Juliet.'

Greg knew he was crazy. She was saying 'please' in a way that no man could possibly misinterpret. He could feel her body yielding to him, feel it softening, opening, the soft little sounds she was making in the back of her throat. No doubt. All he had to do was kiss her and she'd dissolve, crumple up right here on the floor if that was what he wanted.

And still he held back, offering her a way out, giving her a chance to think again.

Why?

She wasn't some nervous virgin who didn't know whether she wanted this or not. He'd never been interested in those. He'd liked women who knew what they wanted and weren't afraid to show him. Juliet was a grown woman and they'd both known where this would end the minute they'd started baiting one another with verbal foreplay.

He had his hands full of hot, sexy womanhood. She knew exactly how he was feeling right now and she wasn't exactly pushing him away. This should have been so damned simple.

But it wasn't.

And he didn't know why.

Except, except…

'I need to know that this is what you want.'

Her response was to lift a hand, lay it along his cheek. She was trembling, he realised. Not with fear, because if she'd been afraid she would have been rigid in his arms, would not have been openly encouraging his mouth on her breasts. She was trembling with desire and knowing that made him feel ten times, a hundred times stronger, more powerful than he'd ever felt in his life. And still he waited, doing nothing to encourage her, nothing to discourage her.

He wanted her to know that despite his sudden lapse into the kind of machismo behaviour that he despised, that was an invitation to any self-respecting woman to show him the door, he was not so lost to his own needs that he wouldn't step back if that was what she wanted.

As if rewarding him for his patience, she lifted her other hand so that she was cradling his face. And then she lifted her mouth to his and kissed him very gently.

It was the sweetest kiss.

The kind that an innocent teenage girl might bestow on her first boyfriend. All soft, trembling lips. Uncertain longings. The kind that would be wasted on a hot, horny youth who had only one thing in mind. The kind that could steal a man's heart. She couldn't begin to imagine how much it cost him to hold back, allow her to take the lead, set the pace. Had no way of understanding that her tenderness was burning him up in a way that not even the hottest of kisses had ever achieved.

Then he realised that her face was wet, that tears were pouring down her cheeks and mingling with their lips. And at that point he knew that he was a fool. This wasn't a game. This was something beyond his imagining and if he couldn't have her, make her his—if not now, then one day when he'd earned her trust—he would surely die.

And remembering his earlier arrogance, his determination that he wasn't getting this close to the lady until she was the one who was pleading with him for fulfilment, he felt utter shame. Knew that at this moment he deserved nothing more than that she step back from her kiss and advise him to call a taxi because the evening was over.

CHAPTER TEN

'JULIET?'

Greg could no longer bear the silence. He was the one begging, on his knees inside his head, if not in reality.

Then in the faint glimmer of light seeping through to the rear of the shop he saw her smile and she said, 'Can you wait for coffee?'

Juliet opened her eyes. She felt reborn. New.

For once in her life she hadn't thought about anyone but herself. Her mother, her tutors, the company...

All her life she'd been trying to please someone else and last night she'd taken the risk, stepped off the edge and taken the decision to please no one but herself.

Above her the hideous black ceiling was blocked out by her beautiful, tender, unbelievably sexy knight, the slayer not just of her playground dragons but of her personal ones too. The low early morning sunlight shimmered off his naked shoulders and, unable to resist touching him, she trailed her fingers along the line of his collar-bone until she reached the little hoop of bone in the centre. Then she changed direction, moving down...

He caught her hand before she could do any serious damage. 'Princess, we have to talk.'

'Do we, McLeod?' she responded archly.

'Damn it, woman, don't start that again. I promise

you, I've never called another woman ''princess'' in my entire life.'

The sun edged behind a cloud.

Let it go, her subconscious warned. She was good at that. Not asking the important questions all her life. Avoiding hurt. Last night all that had changed.

'Never?' she challenged.

'Never,' he responded.

Only someone who knew it to be a lie would have recognised the millisecond pause before he replied for what it was. A man deciding whether to tell the truth or lie. And deciding on the latter.

Why was she surprised? Why did it even matter? It was just a little wriggle of a white lie to cover his slip. To make her feel special. He'd warned her that he wasn't Galahad.

What was the big deal?

He was just one more thing on the 'want/need/do' list of her life, after all. One perfect night in the arms of Gregor McLeod. All right, so that wasn't what she'd written in her notebook, but then she'd only been thirteen. A stupid, romantic, skinny kid who had known no better.

Whatever she'd written then, this was now. Last night had been no more than one more tick on her master plan, another brick in the wall of her ambitions.

So why was her heart crumbling into pieces?

'Juliet, Juliet, Juliet...' He repeated her name, lifting her hand to his lips, kissing her palm, and a quiver of hot desire rippled through her. 'Please——'

'Sorry, McLeod,' she said, never more grateful for the interruption of the shop doorbell. Nothing else would have saved her from the heat of desire burning in his eyes...that at least had been real. 'I'm afraid that's my mother.' And, reclaiming her hand, she flung back the bedclothes and began gathering his scattered clothes. 'She's helping me in the shop today.'

He rolled on to his side to watch her and suddenly she felt naked, exposed...

'I could help too. Then we could talk.'

Talk? Oh, sure, she really believed he wanted to talk.

She dropped his clothes beside him on the bed. 'The, um, debriefing will have to keep, I'm afraid. You're not on my to-do list today.'

He didn't move, watching her as she wrenched open a drawer in her hunt for clean underwear. She gave up on a bra and scrambled into a pair of jeans and a sweat-shirt.

'You've got the top on inside out,' he said.

She was half out of it before she realised that she hadn't. 'Oh, very funny...'

'You can't blame a man for wanting to keep you naked. Tell your mother that something more urgent came up.'

He wasn't even ashamed of himself. He was lying back, his hands behind his head, as if he was planning to stay in her bed all day. To just lie there waiting for her to come back so that they could continue where they'd left off and she felt the warm, heavy drag of desire respond to his arousal. That was the trouble with temptation. Once you'd surrendered to it, it was so much harder to say no. That was why she had to get away. Before she was irretrievably hooked.

'I thought you wanted to talk,' she said, looking away as she hunted for shoes. Anything to take her mind off what her body was telling her.

'I do. We'll fool around a little, talk a little, eat a little... We've got all day.'

'You may have. I've got work to do. Use the back stairs when you leave. They'll take you straight down to the street,' she said. 'Just watch out for Dave's ladders in the lobby. I'm already fully booked for hospital visiting.'

'What's she doing in the shop? Your mother.'

'Just giving me a hand to get it into shape for tomorrow.'

'If there's heavy lifting to be done you'll need me.'

'You're wearing a suit, McLeod.' A very expensive suit. Not that the designer's signature had come as much of a surprise. He rode a Harley, drove a vintage Jaguar, and while she'd never been to a party in a castle she was quite sure that they didn't come cheap. He might work for himself, but it certainly wasn't as an odd job man. Gregor McLeod was a lot more than that. She'd only kept taunting him with it in the hope that he'd tell her what he actually did.

But he hadn't. He'd told her the melt your heart story about his daughter and it had done the job. But he hadn't told her anything about himself. What he did now.

The omission told her everything she needed to know. Not that it mattered.

'I'll go home and change.'

'No!' Then, 'You don't understand. Mum will take one look at you and she'll know…' She swallowed.

'What? That we spent the night together? You're not a kid, Juliet.'

'It isn't that.' He frowned. 'It's just…'

'What?'

Why on earth did she have to explain? He'd got everything he wanted. In her admittedly limited experience hanging around to 'talk' after a night of hot sex was not on most men's agenda.

'I've already made a total mess of my life. She was the one who picked up the pieces and got me moving again. She'll take one look at you and see the kind of man that any sensible, level-headed woman—any *sane* woman—would run a mile from. She'll take one look at you and send for the men in white coats. Let's face it, McLeod, you're bad.'

He pretended to look offended. 'No, I'm not. I'm very, very good. You told me so any number of times last night.' He grinned and, putting on a feminine voice, he said, *'Oh, Gregor. Oh, yes! Oh, you're so gooooood...'*

Juliet blushed. *'Please...'*

'You are totally irresistible when you beg. Did I tell you that?'

'I didn't...'

'You're sure?' And the flash of mischief in his eyes suggested that he was considering a reprise of that too.

'Will you please *go?*' Then, 'This is begging, McLeod. You can't resist, remember?'

'Give me a kiss and I'll think about it.'

'Joo-o-o-ls...' Her mother's insistent call saved her from the temptation. She glanced out of the window and saw her mother standing back from the street door, looking up. 'Are you awake?'

She leaned out and called down, 'Hold on, I'll be right there.' She picked up her keys and avoiding looking at Gregor, she said, 'I've got to go.'

Greg was out of bed and blocking the door before she was halfway across the room.

He was the screw-up, not her, and he wanted her to know that. He'd thought he was so damned clever with

his teasing. Thought this was just a sweet interlude
with someone who, for once, wasn't looking at him as
a meal ticket or wanting a job. He could just relax,
enjoy himself. Help out an old friend and indulge a
pretty woman…

Last night he'd recognised that he was fooling himself. From the first time he'd heard her speak, from the
moment she'd brushed off his come-on with the deri-
sion it deserved, he'd known it was a whole lot more
than that. This was not just another flirtation. This was
different. Being with her, making her happy, was more
important than anything else and he had to tell her that.
Tell her everything.

He had thought he'd have all day to tell her the truth.
Explain. Time between making love to her, sharing
breakfast in bed, cramming once more into a shower
so tiny that the water had barely room to seep between
their bodies.

'Let me go, McLeod.'

Now she was calling him McLeod again. His mistake, calling her princess when she was alert enough
to notice. She hadn't objected when she was so lost to
desire that he'd thought they'd both go up in flames.
In fact, he was sure she didn't mind at all, just enjoyed
the verbal jousting. Was using it now just to distance
herself from him and why would she do that?

'No, just hold on a damn second here. *Jools?*' If he
could just make her laugh… 'I get earache for calling
you ''princess'' and you allow your mother to call you
''Jools''?'

'She's earned the right to call me whatever she
wants. Stand aside, McLeod.'

Not so much as a smile. 'That's it?' he said with a
touch of desperation as he felt something precious slip-

ping away from him. 'Dismissed without so much as a kiss?'

'No kiss,' she said, looking him straight in the face. 'I bought you dinner. All debts are settled in full. Don't make a noise when you leave.'

Nothing had ever sounded more final. More like goodbye.

Then she wasn't looking at him. She wasn't looking anywhere and, as she fumbled for the door handle, she lost her grip on the shoes, dropping one.

They both stooped to pick it up but he was marginally faster and, as he handed it to her, she looked up, her eyes glistening and said, 'Thank you.'

Juliet stumbled down the stairs and unlocked the door, letting her mother in.

'Good grief, Jools, you look terrible.'

'Sorry, I overslept. It was a long night.' Long, beautiful and, inevitably, heartbreaking...

She had fooled herself into believing that a single night would be enough. The temptation of a long, lazy day had shown her just how wrong she had been. It was going to be hard enough to cope with the fallout from this, move on. If she allowed herself to indulge in a whole day spent in Gregor McLeod's arms she would never recover from the pain of losing him. She cleared her throat.

'Do you want to put the kettle on while I go and feed Archie?'

'You're overdoing it, Jools.'

'No, I need to keep busy. I was thinking about putting together a proposal for one of those self-help books for women,' she rattled on quickly, whether to distract her mother or herself she couldn't have said.

'You know, time management for your busy life.' She barely paused for breath. 'And maybe I could do some rather more basic articles for the women's magazines. I've been doing some research...' She would do some research... 'What do you think?'

Apparently reassured, her mother shrugged. 'Maybe you should think about writing a crime novel. One where the woman gets away with murdering a cheating, lying man and takes over the world. I bet that would be a bestseller.'

'Two good ideas in one morning.' She managed a smile. 'I'd better put them on the career-building list before I forget.' She glanced around for her notebook but, in her rush to escape, she'd left it upstairs. 'I'll do it later. Right now we have books to shelve, displays to erect and those two front windows to dress.'

If she wasn't quite busy enough to ignore the pain, at least she didn't have time to take it out and wallow in it.

It was like being hit with a sledgehammer.

Greg didn't move for what seemed an age. He'd known from the start that he'd seen her before. There had been something about her eyes, her voice, even her streaky fair hair—brighter than mouse but not quite blonde—that had tugged at some distant memory.

But she'd been a skinny little kid with hair in a plait that hadn't been pulled tight enough and was falling out around her face. She was being teased by a group of girls who were thirteen going on thirty, with their faces made up and their skirts up to their backsides. They had been all around her, mocking the way she spoke. Trying to escape them, she'd stumbled and fallen, spilling the contents of her bag, and he'd gone to her, had rescued a notebook before it was grabbed by one of the little cats who'd been giving her a hard time. Had helped her gather the rest of her things.

Her eyes had been swimming in tears and she was shaking like a leaf as he'd put the notebook into her hand, but she'd looked up and said, 'Thank you,' so sweetly, so softly.

And he'd said, 'Anytime, princess.'

He had never known her name, had just called her 'princess,' because she had sounded exactly like one. But he'd looked out for her after that, had made certain no one bullied her when he was around.

Dear God, she must have known who he was from the start. Why on earth hadn't she said anything? No, scrub that. Stupid question.

The answer was there in that moment when she'd opened the door. He'd just proclaimed himself her knight errant and had been standing there like a total idiot, pleased with himself, pleased with life, anticipating a warm welcome in return for his good deed; what he'd got had been a long silence. She'd recognised him the moment she'd seen him. And had waited for him to recognise her.

Damn it, but that was completely unreasonable and he'd tell her so right now. She'd had him at a disadvantage, he told himself, as he began to fling on his clothes. He hadn't changed that much. Put on a bit of weight, got a bit older, that was all. Nothing major. Damn it, he'd even been riding a motorbike. She'd have known him anywhere. But Juliet...

His little princess had changed out of all recognition. She was a woman. A beautiful, confident, sexy woman. How was he expected to know that she was that pathetic little kid in the charity shop clothes?

Except that he had known. Not on a conscious level, but somewhere deep inside where memories lurk to trip you up, give you a hard time when you least expect it, he'd known. And, without even thinking about it, he'd called her 'princess.'

She thought he'd lied to her about that. But he hadn't. She was the only one. Would always be the only one. He had to tell her, somehow make her believe it was true.

For that he needed her to listen to him and there was one sure way to grab her attention. He wasted no more time, but dressed, picking up his keys, wallet, notebook from the bedside table before using his phone to summon a taxi to pick him up at the end of the lane. He just hoped his architect had no other plans for the day...

Juliet was exhausted. She'd worked herself to a standstill in an attempt to stop herself from having to think. She was too tired to eat and the trip to the hospital had finished her. When she made it to the top floor flat, she only had the energy to fall into bed. The last thing she remembered thinking was that the sheets smelled of Gregor McLeod. That washing them would be the hardest thing she'd ever done.

'I'll be getting on with the flat now we're done down here, Miss Howard.'

Juliet was in something of a dilemma. Dave had told her that he'd been out of a job when Duke's went bankrupt. That at his age getting another job had been difficult. And clearly, for Maggie's sake, the flat needed decorating as much as the shop had.

But she didn't want to rack up any further 'debts' with McLeod.

There was one more thing he could do for Maggie, though. 'I'd rather you paint the outside of the shop, Dave. If that isn't taking too much advantage of your good nature.' She took him outside. 'Glossy black with gold lettering. Do you know a good sign-writer? Maggie and I have decided to rename the shop Kiss & Kill. It would be nice to have it done by the time she gets out of hospital.'

'Just tell me what you want, Miss Howard, and it'll be done.'

She thought of McLeod's expensive suit and tried not to feel too guilty as she explained.

'Greg? Where are you?'

'Neil, I can't talk right now.'

'Maybe not, but you'd better listen. Marty Duke might have fled the country but he didn't bother to take his wife with him and she's been talking to the press...'

Despite the obstacle of the ladders outside that deterred browsers, Juliet had plenty to do packing up the kind of books they were no longer going to sell in order to return them to the publishers. Packing up the orders that had come in the post. Talking about a Web site for the shop with a friend of Saffy's from the local college.

Putting a poster in the window inviting anyone interested in joining a crime readers group to contact her mother.

After lunch Saffy was despatched to the baker's to pick up the cakes that had been ordered for the romance readers group who were having their monthly meeting that afternoon—for the first time with refreshments.

'Juliet, did your mother once live in Milsom Street?' she asked when she returned.

'Years ago.' Before she'd been born. 'Why do you ask?'

'Someone was looking at the poster in the window and asked me.'

Juliet got up and went through to find a tallish, thinnish, rather elegant man and she offered her hand. 'I'm Juliet Howard. I understand you're asking about my mother.'

He went so pale that she thought he was going to faint, and she quickly ushered him into one of the roomy armchairs that she'd bought from a local second-hand dealer for the front of the shop.

'Saffy, get some water.'

'No, no, I'm fine, really, it's just such a shock. You're so like her.' He shook his head. 'I never thought of her married, with children.'

'I'm sorry?'

'Becky. Becky Howard. She is your mother?' He didn't wait for her answer. 'You carry this picture with you in your head, don't you, of things the way they were? For me she's always been that girl standing on the platform at Melchester Station wearing tight blue jeans and a white T-shirt as she waved me off.'

'You knew my mother?'

'We were both just teenagers. I…I moved away. I wrote with my address as soon as we were settled. She promised she'd write back…'

And that was when she realised that she was looking at her father. That he hadn't deserted her, run away. That he'd never even known she existed. That, far from being deserted by her young lover in her hour of need, her mother had never told him that he had a daughter.

'Where did you go?'

She asked rather more sharply than she'd intended and he looked up. 'Go?'

'When you left Melchester.'

'Oh. Well, Cornwall that time. My father worked for a bank and he was moved whenever he was promoted. I didn't want to go, but we were both still at school. I would have come back, but when she didn't write I thought, well, she's found someone else. It happens doesn't it? Of course we were ridiculously young—'

'Did you? Find someone else?'

'No one who could hold a candle to Becky. No one I could ever imagine being married to, living with...'

'Saffy,' she said, with an outward calmness that belied her inner turmoil. 'Will you please go and telephone my mother? Tell her to drop whatever she's doing and come here. Straight away. And then make some coffee. Or maybe you'd prefer tea...' She could hardly speak. 'I'm sorry, I don't know your name.'

'It's Walker. James Walker. And a cup of tea would be wonderful. Thank you.'

'Jools?' Her mother came through the door in a rush five minutes later. 'What's wrong?'

And then, as she saw the man slowly rising to his feet, she dropped everything she was carrying as her hands flew to her mouth. 'James...' She put out a hand, half withdrew it, and then he was holding it and they were in each other's arms.

Saffy said, 'What on earth is going on?'

'Romance, Saffy. Boy meets girl, boy loses girl, boy finds girl again.' With a broad sweep of her arm she encompassed the new dedicated romance section of the bookstore and said, 'Read all about it...'

Her gaze came to a halt on the newspaper her mother had dropped along with her handbag.

Mystery Developer Named

And beneath the headline was a photograph of Gregor McLeod.

Behind her the bell on the shop door pinged and she knew who it was even before she turned around.

'Juliet...'

'Mr McLeod. To what do we owe the pleasure? Have you come to view the site for your new car park?'

'I tried to get here before you saw that.'

'Why?' She felt extraordinarily calm, or maybe she was simply numb. Too much was happening and, like a computer when the buffer is full, her brain just couldn't handle any more... 'What difference would it have made?'

'I was going to tell you...' He hesitated, glancing at her mother and James who were staring at them both.

'Oh, please, don't be coy. You were going to tell me yesterday morning. Did you think that once you'd got me to bed I would be putty in your hands? That I'd forget all about Prior's Lane and the people who work here? Like your dear friend Maggie?'

The shop seemed very full all of a sudden, but that didn't matter, the more people who heard exactly what kind of a man he was, the better. 'You think you're so damned clever, Mr McLeod. Pretended you weren't interested in what we're doing to save Prior's Lane, but you didn't stop me talking about it, did you? You were always ready with a question if I drifted off topic. You even let me pay for the privilege, you cheapskate.'

'Juliet, please, let me explain…'

She was aware, on some level, that she was behaving very badly. But she'd spent her entire life behaving so very, very well while everyone around her had lied and lied and lied…

'What? Not your princess any more?'

Maybe he realised that there was nothing he could say or do that could begin to explain the depth of his betrayal because he didn't reply.

'No, obviously not. Well, you might think you've won. That I'll just crawl into a hole and stop bothering you, but you're wrong.' She took a step towards him. 'I am done with doing what other people want, done with running away from confrontation, done with being lied to. I will fight you every step of the way.' She jabbed at the soft cashmere overcoat he wearing. 'Do your worst. I will never let you destroy something people value.' She jabbed again because it felt so good to be fighting back.

He caught her hand before she could do it a third time. 'Juliet, I love you.'

She laughed. 'Oh, *please*. Now I know you're desperate.'

As she turned her back on him she realised that there were a dozen or so women standing open-mouthed behind her.

'Are you the romance readers group?' she asked. 'I'm sorry, we're having a really extraordinary day. My long lost father has turned up out of the blue and so has the man who wants to turn this area into a car park.

All it needs is the man who stole my career to turn up and we'll have a full set.'

'Juliet!'

This time it was her mother, but she ignored her too.

'Do you want to go through to the back, ladies? We've tried to make you as comfortable as possible and if you'll just let Saffy know when you want tea or coffee...' Then, because no one seemed to have anything to say, 'If you'll excuse me I just need to go somewhere so that I can scream.'

It didn't take her flight to the top floor to knock all desire to scream out of Juliet. It didn't take her that long to work out that one or all the people she was running from would come after her and she wasn't ready to face any of them.

Sooner, rather than later, she was going to have to apologise for her behaviour to them all—well, most of them—but not yet. Not until she'd had a chance to gather herself, come to terms with betrayal on an unimaginable scale.

She grabbed her coat and bag and took the back stairs that led straight down to the street but when she opened the door she discovered that Gregor had anticipated her flight and was standing on the doorstep, waiting for her. Her only retreat was back up the stairs.

'We need to talk,' he said.

'I haven't got anything to say—'

'But I have. Shall we go upstairs, or would you rather walk?'

'I—I...'

'Let's walk then,' he said, taking the coat she'd grabbed without stopping to put it on, holding it out so that she could slip her arms into the sleeves. 'It's cold,' he said when she resisted his invitation.

She silently submitted before banging the door behind her and striding out along the access alley in the direction of the river, leaving him to follow or not as he chose, saying nothing until she stopped to lean against the parapet of the bridge and catch her breath and blink back the tears that were nothing more than a reaction to the icy air.

Downstream the abandoned warehouses were reflected in the still water and she wished she'd gone in the opposite direction, up towards the cathedral. Something that McLeod could never own.

He caught up with her, handing her a cup of steaming tea he'd stopped to buy at a refreshment stall. 'That was your father? In the bookshop?'

'It would seem so.'

'How do you feel about that?'

She stared at him. He wanted to talk about the unexpected appearance of her father? 'How do you think I feel? My mother lied to me. She told me... let me believe...that he'd walked away. Abandoned her...me.'

'And he didn't?'

'He hadn't got the first clue I existed. When he saw me he thought she'd married someone else...that I was someone else's daughter.' No use pretending about the tears, or trying to hide them as she turned to him. 'Why would she do that?'

'You could ask her.' He shrugged. 'Or maybe use your imagination. They must have both been very young.'

'Still at school. Something you'd know all about.'

'Yes, well, maybe she wanted him to be free to

achieve all he was capable of. Maybe she loved him that much. If he'd known, nothing would have kept him away.'

'How do you know that?'

'Because if I'd been left in ignorance my daughter would feel the same way about me as you do about him.'

'And you think Fiona was thinking of your future when she kept silent?'

'I know that Fiona was thinking entirely about herself, but then we weren't in love.'

She sipped the tea and grimaced. 'You've put sugar in this.'

'I thought you could probably do with it.' Then, 'I didn't lie to you, Juliet.'

'You didn't tell me the truth.'

He stared down the river. 'When I called you "princess" it was purely instinctive.'

She frowned. That wasn't what she'd been talking about and he knew it...

'It's not an endearment I use casually, although I don't blame you for thinking it. The truth is that I have used it once before. There was this skinny little kid at school. Silver-grey eyes too big for her face...' As she shivered he took his scarf and wrapped it around her neck before wiping a thumb across her cheek. 'They were full of tears too.'

'Gregor...'

'She'd dropped her bag and I picked up some of her stuff.' He took something from his pocket and held up a scuffed black notebook. 'This notebook.'

Juliet swallowed. 'I wondered what had happened to that,' she said, not taking it.

'I picked it up yesterday morning by mistake,' he

said, placing it beside her on the stone parapet. 'I have one very like it.'

'I know. You wrote down the measurements for the glass in it.' Then, 'I—I suppose you've read it?'

'If I was a true knight errant, a perfect Galahad, I'd have resisted the temptation. I never pretended to be either.'

'No.'

'It's an impressive document. You had a very clear idea of what you wanted and you've achieved pretty much everything you set out to do.'

'I'm very disciplined. Shame about the directorship.'

'I'm far more concerned that most of the unticked ambitions are on the fun side of the list. I think you should spend some time filling in the gaps.'

On the contrary, she'd made a fairly impressive start when she'd spent the night with him, but this didn't seem the right moment to mention it so she said, 'Should I start with the spiky hairdo?'

'You have lovely hair...' Then, 'But if it's what you want, why not?'

'No, I never really wanted that. I just wanted to be like everyone else.'

'No reason to miss out on the trip to Disney in Paris, though. I've never been either.'

'I'm saving that up until I have at least four children of my own to take with me.'

'I noticed the four children on your master plan. If you don't mind me saying so, Juliet, you're not getting any younger. You need to start work on that in the very near future—'

'Thank you for that.'

'—and as the chosen father I'm happy to cooperate any time you say, although I'd have to insist that you make an honest man of me and marry me first.' Until then he'd been so serious, but without warning his eyes creased in the kind of smile that could get a woman into all kinds of trouble. 'That's not an offer I make lightly, Juliet. In fact it's a first for me.'

'The children, or the marriage?'

'Both.'

She tried to resist the softening of her mouth, to stop her eyes from betraying her feelings.

'Thanks, McLeod, but it'll take more than the promise of four children and a trip to Disney to make me forget about your plans for Prior's Lane.'

'Did anyone ever tell you that you set impossibly high standards in knights errant, princess?'

'Would you expect any less from the mother of your future children, McLeod?'

'Nothing less,' he admitted. 'Maybe if I showed you what I had in mind for that part of the city you'd reconsider my offer?'

He didn't wait for her to agree but reached into his coat and took a long envelope from the inside pocket, spreading out the contents for her to see. 'It's just an artist's impression, of course,' he said. 'Hilliard dashed it off for me yesterday. I've asked him to work with you on it.'

She stared at the sketch of Prior's Lane looking exactly as she'd imagined it, even down to the elegant wrought-iron roof protecting the shoppers from the elements.

'I don't know what to say, Gregor.'

'Yes?' he suggested as he folded up the drawing and handed it to her.

'Yes?'

'Well, if you say no, I might as well build a car park after all.'

'What? But that's blackmail.'

'You said it…I'm bad.'

And suddenly she couldn't stop the smile from breaking out all over her face. 'Maybe I was a little harsh, although…'

'There's more?'

'Well, I've been thinking about Duke's Yard. There are a lot of good men out of work and it seemed to me that if they had somewhere where they could set up as a sort of cooperative with an office manager to organise the paperwork…?'

'Only if you organise it.'

'I can do that.'

'I didn't doubt it for a moment, but there is just one more thing we need to settle.'

'Oh?'

He took a torn credit card slip from his pocket and handed it to her.

'What's this?'

'Just a little reassurance that if you say yes to all of the above you won't be marrying a cheapskate.'

She stared at the receipt, then at him, and as he gathered her into his arms there was no need for words. Her lips were saying yes, yes, yes more eloquently, more fervently than any affirmative listed in the dictionary. Which was maybe why neither of them heard the splash as a small black notebook fell from the parapet of the bridge, hit the water and then sank without trace.

'What's this? More fan mail for the new arrival?'

Juliet looked up at her husband as he gazed adoringly at the infant lying in the cradle beside her and bit back a smile at the sight of so much power laid low by such a tiny bundle of pink and white.

'There's a card from Chloe, full of heartfelt thanks for providing her with a baby sister at last. She's coming down at the weekend to drool in person...' She handed him the note so that he could read it for himself. 'There's a postcard from Mum and Dad too, presumably sent before they rushed back from their honeymoon. I feel so guilty about that.'

'There's nothing to stop them having another one any time they like. Is that a card from Maggie?'

'I do hope she's not overdoing it.'

'Jimmy's taking good care of her.'

'Um. I don't suppose it's a coincidence that the perfect job just happened to fall into his lap on the redevelopment project, is it?'

'It's what friends are for. What's that?'

'This?' She held up a letter written on heavy cream stationery. 'Just a note from Lord Markham asking me if I'd be prepared to join the board of Markham and Ridley. For some reason the shareholders seem to have been unimpressed with the nepotism of his last appointment.'

'Just another day in paradise then? How much are they offering?'

'Twice what they could have had me for if they'd been smart.'

'Tempted?'

'Not even remotely.' She let the letter fall to the floor as she lifted her baby girl from her cradle and tucked her into her father's arms. Then, leaning forward to kiss him, she said, 'I've got all I ever wanted right here.'

If you enjoyed what you just read,
then we've got an offer you can't resist!

Take 2 bestselling
love stories FREE!
Plus get a FREE surprise gift!

Clip this page and mail it to Harlequin Reader Service®

IN U.S.A.	IN CANADA
3010 Walden Ave.	P.O. Box 609
P.O. Box 1867	Fort Erie, Ontario
Buffalo, N.Y. 14240-1867	L2A 5X3

YES! Please send me 2 free Harlequin Romance® novels and my free surprise gift. After receiving them, if I don't wish to receive anymore, I can return the shipping statement marked cancel. If I don't cancel, I will receive 6 brand-new novels every month, before they're available in stores! In the U.S.A., bill me at the bargain price of $3.57 plus 25¢ shipping & handling per book and applicable sales tax, if any*. In Canada, bill me at the bargain price of $4.05 plus 25¢ shipping & handling per book and applicable taxes**. That's the complete price and a savings of 10% off the cover prices—what a great deal! I understand that accepting the 2 free books and gift places me under no obligation ever to buy any books. I can always return a shipment and cancel at any time. Even if I never buy another book from Harlequin, the 2 free books and gift are mine to keep forever.

186 HDN DZ72
386 HDN DZ73

Name	(PLEASE PRINT)	
Address	Apt.#	
City	State/Prov.	Zip/Postal Code

Not valid to current Harlequin Romance® subscribers.
Want to try another series? Call 1-800-873-8635
or visit www.morefreebooks.com.

* Terms and prices subject to change without notice. Sales tax applicable in N.Y.
** Canadian residents will be charged applicable provincial taxes and GST.
All orders subject to approval. Offer limited to one per household.
® are registered trademarks owned and used by the trademark owner and or its licensee.

HROM04R   ©2004 Harlequin Enterprises Limited

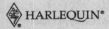